MURDER

AT

BLACK OAKS

ALSO BY PHILLIP MARGOLIN

Heartstone
The Last Innocent Man
Gone, But Not Forgotten
After Dark
The Burning Man
The Undertaker's Widow
The Associate
Sleeping Beauty
Lost Lake
Worthy Brown's Daughter
Woman with a Gun
Vanishing Acts (with Ami Margolin Rome)

AMANDA JAFFE NOVELS
Wild Justice
Ties That Bind
Proof Positive
Fugitive
Violent Crimes

DANA CUTLER NOVELS
Executive Privilege
Supreme Justice
Capitol Murder
Sleight of Hand

ROBIN LOCKWOOD NOVELS
The Third Victim
The Perfect Alibi
A Reasonable Doubt
A Matter of Life and Death
The Darkest Place

MURDER AT BLACK OAKS

A ROBIN LOCKWOOD NOVEL

Phillip Margolin

St. Martin's Paperbacks

This is a work of fiction. All of the characters, organizations, and events portrayed in this novel are either products of the author's imagination or are used fictitiously.

Published in the United States by St. Martin's Paperbacks, an imprint of St. Martin's Publishing Group

MURDER AT BLACK OAKS

Copyright © 2022 by Phillip Margolin.
Excerpt from *Betrayal* copyright © 2023 by Phillip Margolin.

For information, address St. Martin's Publishing Group, 120 Broadway, New York, NY 10271.

www.stmartins.com

Library of Congress Catalog Card Number: 2022027255

ISBN: 978-1-250-89641-4

Our books may be purchased in bulk for promotional, educational, or business use. Please contact your local bookseller or the Macmillan Corporate and Premium Sales Department at 1-800-221-7945, ext. 5442, or by email at MacmillanSpecialMarkets@macmillan.com.

Printed in the United States of America

Minotaur hardcover edition published 2022
St. Martin's Paperbacks edition / November 2023

10 9 8 7 6 5 4 3 2 1

When I was in elementary school and junior high school I devoured the novels of Ellery Queen, Agatha Christie, John Dickson Carr, and other great mystery writers. Murder at Black Oaks *is an homage to all of the great writers from the Golden Age of mysteries who inspired me to write a novel with an impossible murder, a haunted mansion, secret passages, and a werewolf curse, the wonderful ingredients that made those old mysteries so great.*

PART ONE

THE ATTORNEY-CLIENT PRIVILEGE

CHAPTER ONE

1990

In order for an Oregon Circuit Court judge to sentence a defendant charged with aggravated murder to death, all twelve members of a defendant's jury had to answer yes to several questions. Those questions asked whether the defendant deliberately killed the victim without justifiable provocation, whether there was a probability that the defendant would commit acts of violence in the future, and whether, given all the circumstances in the case, the jurors thought the defendant should be sentenced to death.

As soon as the foreperson of the jury in the sentencing phase of Jose Alvarez's capital murder case told Judge Muriel Jacobs that the jurors had unanimously found against Jose Alvarez, Judge Jacobs took a deep breath. Facing her with a stunned expression was a twenty-four-year-old college student whose bright future had turned to ashes.

Judge Jacobs took a sip of water before speaking. When she did speak, it took an effort to appear calm. This was the first time she had to impose a sentence of death, and she felt sick.

"Mr. Alvarez, you have just heard that the jurors have unanimously decided that the punishment in your case should be a sentence of death. Since they have reached this verdict, the law gives me no choice but to remand you to the custody of the Department of Corrections, where you will remain until a sentence of death has been carried out. Your attorney will advise you about your recourse at law."

Jose stared at the judge. His legs shook, and he had to brace himself on the counsel table to stay upright.

"Please, Judge. I would never hurt Margo. Don't do this."

"I have no choice, Mr. Alvarez. Once your jurors reached its decision my hands were tied. I'm sorry."

And the judge was genuinely sorry. Even though she was convinced that Alvarez had murdered his girlfriend, she would not have condemned the young man to death.

Jose collapsed onto his seat. In the spectators' section, Jose's parents began to cry. They were immigrants who had dedicated their lives to giving their brilliant son an education. He had repaid them by graduating near the top of his high school class and maintaining a straight-A average in engineering at an elite college. Now the object of all their energy would rot on death row until he was put down with a lethal injection.

Frank Melville watched Jose's attorney lay a comforting hand on his client's shoulder. The deputy district attorney knew that Jose's lawyer was telling Jose that they would appeal, that his death at the hands of the State was not a foregone conclusion. Frank knew that Jose's life would not be saved by the Oregon Supreme Court. The trial had been very clean, and there were no errors in the record that would lead to a new trial.

Frank put the file on the Alvarez case in his attaché case. He was relieved that his role in this tragedy was over. When the young district attorney had won his other capital cases, he had felt proud that he had avenged a killer's victim, but he wasn't experiencing the same jolt of electricity now.

Frank hefted his attaché case and walked through the bar of the court. He had taken a few steps up the aisle when Jose's parents blocked his way. They didn't look angry. They looked bewildered. Frank knew from the police reports that Pablo and Maria Alvarez were in their midfifties, but they looked frail and much older. Frank had no idea how they had looked before Jose's arrest, but he was certain that Jose's ordeal had aged them.

"Please," Maria begged, "do not do this to our son."

The court guards saw what was happening and walked between Frank and Jose's parents.

Frank wanted to say something, but the finest orator

in the district attorney's office was lost. Frank mumbled, "I'm sorry," and walked toward the courtroom door, fighting the impulse to race into the corridor.

Several deputy district attorneys had been in the spectator section to hear the verdict. As soon as the foreperson delivered it, most of them went upstairs to tell everyone about Frank's latest victory. When Frank walked toward his office, everyone stood up and clapped. Melville ducked his head and raised his hand halfway to acknowledge the applause before closing his office door and dropping onto the chair behind his desk.

Frank appreciated the applause, but he had mixed emotions about the sentence the judge had imposed. Jose Alvarez had proclaimed his innocence when he testified, but Melville had no doubts, reasonable or otherwise, that Alvarez had bludgeoned Margo Prescott to death in her dorm room at Randolph College, where they were students. Several witnesses had seen the couple quarreling shortly before the murder. Archie Stallings had testified that he had seen Jose run from the scene with blood on his clothes. Jose's bloody handprint had been discovered on Prescott's body, and the victim's blood was found on Alvarez's clothing.

Melville *had* given Alvarez a way out. He'd offered to drop the possibility of a death sentence if Alvarez pled to life with the possibility of parole. Alvarez had rejected the offer, so he'd made his choice. Why, then, did Frank feel deflated instead of ecstatic? Was he worried that subconscious bias had played a part in the jury's decision to execute a poor Hispanic who was dating a rich, white coed? Would the jury have spared Alvarez if he had been an upper-class WASP like Archie Stallings and his victim had been a poor Mexican?

Frank had used his exceptional oratorical skills to convince the jurors to vote for death, but now that he'd done his duty, he wondered if he'd done the right thing. Frank sighed. There was no profit in second-guessing. What was done, was done. The odds were against the death sentence being carried out, anyway. Alvarez would have an automatic appeal to the Oregon Supreme Court. Post-conviction review would follow. Then there would be federal appeals and on and on. There were even rumors that the governor was going to order a moratorium on death sentences. Hell, it was almost impossible to get executed in Oregon. There were convicts who had been on death row for decades.

Melville closed his eyes and massaged his eyelids. He was exhausted. Trying a death penalty case took everything out of you. When he opened his eyes, he looked at his watch. It was four o'clock, and there was no way he would be able to concentrate on his other cases. He needed to go home, hug his wife, and slug down a stiff drink.

The young DA put the Alvarez files and trial book on the center of his desk, turned out the lights, and left for home.

* * *

The house in Portland's West Hills where Frank Melville lived was not one that Frank could have afforded on a deputy district attorney's salary. The four-thousand-square-foot Tudor home had been a wedding gift from his wife's parents.

During his second year in law school, Larry Trent, Frank's best friend, had fixed him up with Katherine Whitlow and they had fallen madly in love. Frank knew that Katherine had just returned from a year in England, where she had studied European history at Oxford. He didn't know that she was the sole heir to a fortune until they had been dating for nine months and she finally invited him to her parents' thirty-million-dollar estate in California. Frank's parents were middle-class and he had worked to pay for college and law school. He'd never seen anything like the estate, which wasn't even the Whitlows' primary residence. The Melvilles' "summer home" had been a cabin they rented one week a year on a lake outside of Bend in Central Oregon.

Katherine's father was a self-made man whose fortune had been made when logging was the main industry in Oregon, and he'd taken to Frank right away. Katherine had never made the difference in their net worth an issue and the couple were as much in love now as they had been during their courtship.

Katherine knew that the jury was going to deliver its verdict in the sentencing phase of the Alvarez trial and she met Frank at the front door.

"What happened?" she asked when she saw that her husband was not smiling.

"The jury voted for death."

Katherine frowned. "Why aren't you happy?"

Frank shook his head. "I'm not sure I did the right thing when I argued for the death penalty."

"You told me that you thought he was guilty."

"Oh, he killed Prescott. It's just . . ."

Frank shook his head again. Katherine wrapped her arms around him and he laid his cheek against hers.

"I love you," Frank said.

"Ditto," Katherine answered as she hugged him tighter.

Frank pulled back. "Hey, watch out. You're squashing Frank Junior."

"You mean Nelly Melville."

Frank patted Katherine's stomach, where her baby bump had just started to show.

"That's definitely a boy."

"You wish," Katherine said. Then they kissed again and Katherine steered Frank toward the stairs that led to their bedroom.

"Get changed and I'll get dinner."

"Okay," Frank said, smiling because he knew that he was the luckiest man in the whole wide world.

By the time Frank came down to dinner, the fate of Jose Alvarez was only a faint source of discomfort. By the end of the next week, he was deep into the prosecution of a gangbanger who had murdered a rival gang member and Jose was a distant memory.

CHAPTER TWO

1997

After the Alvarez case, Frank started losing enthusiasm for his work, and two years after Jose Alvarez was sentenced to death, Frank Melville left his job at the Multnomah County district attorney's office for a partnership in the law firm of his old friend Lawrence Trent.

Frank found that he had a knack for personal injury work and he felt good every time he got a judgment for someone who needed the money to help them on the road to recovery from an accident.

Frank also took on the occasional criminal case. The reputation for excellence he had earned as the top prosecutor in the DA's office brought many potential criminal clients to Trent and Melville, and the money he was making allowed him the luxury of being able to pick and choose who he would represent.

The day Frank's life began its descent into hell started on a high note. Frank dropped Nelly Melville off at her school on her second week in first grade. He beamed as he saw her two best friends race up to her and escort his daughter inside, and he smiled all the way to his office.

After spending his time in the trenches at the DA's office, where the horrible and the bizarre were commonplace, it took a lot to surprise Frank, but he was genuinely surprised when his receptionist told him that Archie Stallings was in the waiting room. Frank had not seen Stallings since thanking him after his testimony in the guilt phase of Jose Alvarez's trial, and he wondered why his star witness wanted to see him.

When Frank walked into reception, he almost didn't recognize Stallings. In college, Archie had been on the tennis team and looked like an athlete. His thick chestnut-brown hair would often fall across his brow; there had been a twinkle in his eye, and he projected a look of boyish charm.

Seven years later, Archie didn't look so good. He'd put on weight around his middle, his face was fleshy, and he was going prematurely bald. But the grin was still in place, and he stood and flashed it when Frank walked over.

"Hi, Mr. Melville."

"Hello, Archie. What's up?"

The grin faded. "I'd rather not talk about it here."

"Of course. Follow me back to my office."

Frank settled behind his desk, and Stallings took a client chair. He looked uncomfortable.

"What are you doing now?" Frank asked to break the ice.

"I'm a financial advisor with the Macklin Fund. I've been there two years." Stallings forced a smile. "I'm doing okay business wise, but not so good otherwise."

"Oh?"

"Yeah, well, I got married my senior year. I met Audrey at the Westmont," he said.

The Westmont was Oregon's most exclusive country club, and Frank and Katherine were members.

"Audrey filed for divorce six months ago. Then this bitch . . ." Stallings caught himself. "I guess I shouldn't call her that. Her name is Jane Emery. She's another analyst. She'd been coming on to me, and we went out a few times. Now she's gotten me in big trouble." Stallings shook his head. "My boss told me that they'd have to let me go if I didn't straighten out this mess."

Melville frowned. "I'm not following you."

Stallings leaned forward and looked Frank in the eye.

"We had consensual sex. It was in her place. She invited me up. Now, she's saying I raped her. They arrested me at my office. It was humiliating. My dad got his lawyer on it pronto, and I'm out on bail, but my dad's lawyer doesn't do criminal, and you're the best."

"Tell me what happened after you were arrested."

"The detective was a real asshole. He kept calling me a spoiled rich kid, as if Jane's family didn't have big bucks. And he made the cuffs tight, and he threatened me. Said he thought guys who raped women were pieces of shit. He kept on telling me I'd find out how rape felt when I was in the penitentiary. I've never been so scared."

"What did you say?"

"I watch a lot of law shows on TV, so I knew I had to keep my cool and my mouth shut. You don't have to worry about me. I didn't rape Jane, and I didn't say anything that could be used against me."

"That's good."

"So, Mr. Melville, will you take my case, because I really need the best."

"Let's talk business before we go any further. Defending a case like this could be very expensive."

Frank told Stallings what he'd need as a retainer and how much more expensive things could get if they had to go to trial.

"The money's no problem. Dad's good for it. You give me a figure, and I'll have a check to you tomorrow."

"Okay," Frank said. Then he took a legal pad out of his desk. "Let's get going."

CHAPTER THREE

Archie Stallings was convinced that hiring Frank Melville was one of the smartest things he had ever done. Archie knew that he had been great on the stand and might have won the case on his own, but it was Frank's cross-examination that closed the deal. By the time Frank finished his cross of Jane Emery there wasn't a single juror who wasn't on Archie's side. Frank had convinced every one of them that Emery had seduced Archie, then lied about the rape so she could take over his accounts at his firm. Archie's employer must have been convinced too, because Jane was fired a week after the not-guilty verdict, and Archie received apologies and a promotion.

When Frank heard what happened to Archie's accuser, he was so upset that he stayed home from work for a week. He told the office that he had the flu, but the truth was that he was heartbroken, and he couldn't tell anyone why.

Archie had hugged Frank when the verdict was announced, and Archie's father had shaken his hand. Frank noticed that Archie's mother didn't seem happy, but he was too busy to give that much thought.

Frank and Archie had gone back to his office to wrap up a few matters, and that's when Frank's nightmare began.

"That cross was so beautiful," Archie said when they were in the office with the door closed. "The bitch didn't know what hit her."

Frank didn't like Archie using that term, but he realized that his client was hyped up after his victory.

"I was disappointed when she didn't cry. The cunt sure shed plenty of tears when I smacked her."

"What?"

Stallings smiled. "You know, I wasn't surprised that I had the jury fooled, but I am really surprised that you believed me. I thought you were smarter than that."

"You raped Emery?"

Stallings flashed a wolfish grin. "Most definitely. And she wasn't my first." Stallings shook his head. "I don't regret much in my life, but you'll be shocked when you hear my biggest regret."

Frank was too stunned to speak.

"Remember Margo Prescott? I sure do." Stallings shook his head. "I'd been trying to get in her pants for half a semester, but Alvarez beat me to it. The night she bought it I saw her headed for her dorm. She was crying. I pretended to be sympathetic, and I gave her a shoulder to cry on.

"Poor Margo. Her folks didn't like her dating a

wetback, so they put a lot of pressure on her, and she caved and broke up with Jose. Now she was regretting it.

"I saw my chance, and I escorted her to her room. When I thought the time was right, I made my move, but I miscalculated, and she started to scream." Stallings shrugged. "I couldn't have that so I slugged her. That's when she threatened to tell the cops. There was a picture of Mount Hood she was going to hang on her wall. There were nails and a hammer next to it. I grabbed the hammer and . . . Well, you know what happened next, because you read the medical examiner's report.

"Then my luck almost ran out. I took off and got out of the room seconds before Alvarez came in. Those barrio boys can fight, and he probably would have kicked my ass if he'd caught me standing over his sweetie with that hammer in my hand."

Stallings paused and considered that ancient situation. "The hammer might have evened things up, and I'd have had the element of surprise, but who knows."

Stallings laughed. "Everything did come out okay, though. I'm living the good life, and Alvarez is on death row."

Frank stared at his client. "Jose was innocent?"

"As the driven snow."

"You've got to tell the authorities."

Stallings threw his head back and laughed. "You're kidding, right? I mean, why would I do that?"

The color drained from Frank's face. "What kind of man are you?"

Stallings didn't look offended. "I'm a superior man. If you need proof, consider the fact that I have done many things most people would consider to be very, very bad. And yet I have never been punished. That's because I am so much smarter than most people. If I want something, I don't worry. I don't look at the pros and cons, I take it. Let's face it, Frank, there are shepherds and sheep, mutts and alpha dogs." Stallings shrugged. "God made me what I am, and I enjoy every minute."

"I'm going to the DA."

Stallings smiled and shook his head.

"No, you're not. Do you think I would have made this little speech if I was worried that you'd tattle? You took a course in evidence in law school, right? I bet you got an A. Do you remember the lesson on the attorney-client privilege? In order to assure a client that he can be completely honest with his attorney, whatever a client tells his mouthpiece is confidential, and the lawyer is forbidden to tell anyone what his client told him; not the DA, not his wife, not his bridge partners, nobody.

"And, if you try anything, I'll deny I confessed, and I'll see that you are disbarred. Capisce?"

"Why are you telling me this?"

Stallings shrugged. Then he smiled. "I bet you think I'm a real jerk for making you feel guilty about Mr. Alvarez, and you're probably right. I probably should have kept my mouth shut and not given you something to worry about. Especially after you won my trial. But I act without thinking sometimes, and this is one of them." Stallings grinned. "My bad."

Then he looked at his watch. "Oops, time flies. I've got to meet my folks at a very nice French restaurant. We're celebrating your brilliant win. I was supposed to invite you, but something tells me you'd turn me down. I guess that right about now, you don't have much of an appetite."

Stallings left, and Frank stared at the wall. He felt as if he might throw up. He had to tell somebody that Jose Alvarez was innocent, but he had no way to prove it unless Archie Stallings confessed, and he knew that would never happen. Stallings was a monster, and Frank was going to have to spend the rest of his life knowing that a decent young man was rotting away on death row.

PART TWO

WEREWOLVES

THIRTY YEARS LATER

CHAPTER FOUR

Robin Lockwood and her fiancé, Jeff Hodges, were standing side by side in an elevator. Robin held up her hand and admired her engagement ring. She couldn't help smiling every time she looked at it. Jeff laughed. He was six foot two with shaggy, reddish-blond hair that Robin ran her hands through when they made love.

"You are so silly," Jeff said.

Robin leaned over and kissed Jeff just as the car stopped and the elevator door opened. The couple turned. A man was standing outside the car. He was holding a gun. Robin screamed, "No," and held out the hand with the ring. That's when the man fired, and Robin jerked up in bed, her heart pounding and her eyes wide open, drenched in sweat, and more tired than she'd been when she went to bed.

This was not the first night Robin had been dragged into a nightmare-filled sleep, but this evening her nightmare had been exceptionally vivid. That was probably because this was the two-year anniversary of the day a grief-stricken husband had accidentally gunned down Jeff at the sentencing hearing of another man who'd raped his wife.

Ever since Jeff had been killed, Robin had experienced vivid flashbacks that forced her to relive the unbearable grief she'd suffered, leaving her torn between a desire to have the pain stop and the fear that Jeff would vanish if it did.

Robin was five foot eight with a wiry build, clear blue eyes, a straight nose, high cheekbones, and short blond hair. She'd been a nationally ranked, mixed martial arts fighter in college, and she'd had a brief star turn as "Rockin' Robin" when she fought on TV in pay-per-view bouts, but she'd quit fighting professionally in her first year at Yale Law School after she had suffered a brutal knockout that resulted in a concussion and short-term memory loss.

After moving to Portland, Oregon, to join the firm that had become Barrister, Berman, and Lockwood, Robin stayed in shape by going to McGill's gym every workday morning to spar or pump iron before going to her office.

This morning, Robin didn't want to work out, but she knew she had to keep to her routine or risk falling into despair, so she got her breathing under control, fought back her tears, got into her workout gear, and ran to McGill's.

Portland's Pearl District had been a dusty, decaying area, home to warehouses and populated by the homeless. Then the developers moved in and replaced the grimy, run-down warehouses with gleaming, high-end condos, trendy restaurants, and chic boutiques. McGill's gym took up the bottom floor of one of the few brick buildings that had escaped gentrification. It was dimly lit, smelled of sweat, and was home to professional boxers, MMA fighters, and serious bodybuilders.

Barry McGill had been a top middleweight many pounds ago and was one of Robin's favorite people.

"Your buddy's been here for half an hour, working out, while your sorry ass was still in bed," McGill said.

Robin was certain that Barry knew what day this was, and she was grateful that he was his usual abrasive self and hadn't mentioned Jeff or offered her condolences.

Robin walked over to the mat where Sally Martinez was waiting. Sally was a CPA, but she'd been a championship wrestler in college, who had just missed out on a spot on an Olympic team. After graduating, Sally had studied mixed martial arts. She was a few pounds heavier than Robin, but Robin had a few inches on her friend and they were pretty even in ability, although Robin had a slight edge.

"Sorry I'm late," Robin said.

"Not a problem. I don't have anything pressing at the office."

Sally knew that this was the anniversary of Jeff's death, and she came at Robin extra hard so her friend would be forced to focus. Robin was able to forget Jeff for an hour. Then the workout ended, and the two friends went into the locker room to change.

There were two shower stalls in the ladies' locker room. Robin stripped and went into one of them. As soon as she was alone, memories of Jeff cascaded over her. Robin turned on the shower, hoping that the din of the rushing water would drown out the sound of the sobs that made her chest heave and her heart hurt.

Robin heard Sally's shower stop, but she stayed in her stall. She didn't want her friend to see her like this. She didn't want pity, and she didn't want to burden anyone else with her pain.

"I'm headed out," Sally yelled.

"See you," Robin managed.

A few minutes after Sally left, Robin gathered herself and wiped away her tears. After she dried off, Robin put on the pants suit she kept in her locker and started the twenty-minute walk to her office.

The weather fit Robin's mood. It had rained last night, and there was still a threat of rain in the air. Robin stopped for a latte and a scone at the coffee shop across from her office before taking the elevator to the offices of Barrister, Berman, and Lockwood.

Regina Barrister had been widely recognized as the best criminal lawyer in Oregon. Just before she retired after the onset of dementia, Regina had promoted Mark Berman and Robin to partnerships in the firm and left her practice in their hands.

Mark had graciously let Robin have Regina's corner office, which had spectacular views of the snow-capped peaks of Mount Hood and Mount St. Helens and the Willamette River, but today dark clouds hid the mountains from sight, and the rain was keeping most boats off the river.

Robin had hurt her shoulder when Sally executed a judo throw, and it was still aching when she closed the door to her office. She had just started to check her emails when her receptionist told her that she had a call.

"This is Robin Lockwood. How can I help you?"

"My name is Nelly Melville, and I'm calling for my father, Frank Melville. He has a legal matter he'd like to discuss with you."

"When would he like to come in?"

"That's the thing, Miss Lockwood. My father was in a terrible car accident several years ago. Katherine, his wife and my mother, was killed, and he was paralyzed from the waist down. He hasn't left Black Oaks since he got out of the hospital. It would be extremely difficult for my father to visit your office. Can you come here?"

"Where is Black Oaks?"

"It's on the top of Solitude Mountain, several hours from Portland. We're quite isolated, but the view is spectacular, and I think you'll find Black Oaks interesting. It's a re-creation of a famous manor house that's on the English moors. We've even got a curse attached to the place."

Robin was intrigued. "What does your father want to discuss with me?"

"I don't know. He refused to explain why he wants to see you. Whatever it is has really upset him. I know this is an imposition, but I assure you that you'll be well compensated for your time."

"Can you tell me a little more about your father?"

"You might have heard of him. I know you practice criminal law. He was one of the top prosecutors in the Multnomah County district attorney's office before he went into partnership with Lawrence Trent."

"I'm relatively new to Oregon, so the name doesn't ring a bell."

"Oh, if you haven't been here long, you probably wouldn't know Dad."

For a while, Robin had been able to dull the pain of losing Jeff by immersing herself in a few challenging cases, but her current caseload offered little mental stimulation. The mysterious summons had piqued her interest and going to Black Oaks would take her away from all the sights that were a constant reminder of Jeff.

"I can drive up Wednesday. Is that okay?"

"Thank you. My father will be very grateful. When you get close, phone the house." Nelly gave Robin the number of her cell and the Black Oaks landline. "Cell phone reception is spotty on the mountain, but there's a call box at the gate. Use it if your call doesn't go through. Oh, and pack a bag. You'll probably want to stay the night rather than drive back to Portland, but we have plenty of guest rooms and an excellent cook."

As soon as Robin disconnected, she used the intercom to summon Loretta Washington, one of her associates. Loretta was a five-foot-one, African American dynamo, with eyes the color of milk chocolate, who had recently started to style her hair in cornrows. Robin had nicknamed Loretta "The Flash," because she was always in motion.

Like Robin, Loretta was the first person in her family to graduate from college. She'd grown up in the Bronx, graduated from Queens College in New York, and traveled to Portland when she received a full ride from Lewis & Clark Law School. Loretta's hire had nothing to do with diversity. She had finished fifth in her class, had clerked on the Oregon Supreme Court, and was not only a brilliant appellate attorney but was showing promise as a trial lawyer. She was also fun to be around.

"What's up, boss?" Loretta asked as soon as she settled into a client chair across from Robin.

"I need you to tell me everything you can find out about a man named Frank Melville. He was a DA in Portland and a partner in Lawrence Trent's law firm. A few years ago, he was in a very bad car accident. His wife died, and he was seriously injured. He's wheelchair-bound, and he lives in Black Oaks on Solitude Mountain."

"Sounds spooky."

Robin smiled. "It does, doesn't it? An isolated mansion called Black Oaks on the top of a mountain named Solitude. That's right out of one of those old B movies that starred Bela Lugosi and Boris Karloff."

Loretta's brow furrowed. "Who?"

Jeff had been a movie buff, and he'd insisted that Robin watch *Dracula, Frankenstein, The Wolf Man,* and a raft of black-and-white horror classics.

"Look them up too. Consider it a part of your education."

"How soon do you need this? I'm knee-deep in the research in the *Kim* case."

"Pull yourself out of that quagmire and hop on this. I'm driving up Wednesday, so I need the info ASAP."

"I'll have it to you when you get in tomorrow."

CHAPTER FIVE

By the time Robin went to bed, she was emotionally exhausted and had a deep, dream-free sleep. She felt a little better when she woke up, but her shoulder was still bothering her, so she decided to skip the gym.

Robin was excited about her mysterious mission to Black Oaks, and she was anxious to hear what Loretta had discovered. Her associate was waiting for Robin when Robin walked into her office the next morning carrying two lattes and two croissants.

"What do you know about werewolves?" Loretta asked after taking a bite of her croissant and a sip of the latte.

"Other than what I learned watching those old horror movies, not a lot."

"Then you better get up to speed if you're going to Black Oaks."

"And that is because . . . ?"

Loretta scooted up to the edge of her chair and leaned forward.

"Black Oaks is cursed. Everyone who has lived there has met a horrible end."

Robin smiled. "They get eaten by werewolves?"

"A few have, which should worry you."

Robin laughed. "You have my attention, Loretta. Please go on."

"In 1673, Angus McTavish built Black Oaks on a desolate part of the moors, several miles from Sexton, a small English village. McTavish had two sons. His wife and the youngest boy died from a plague that ravaged the area. Niles, the eldest son, began a career in the clergy, but was defrocked a year into his first posting. McTavish was the wealthiest man in the area, and the reasons for Niles's expulsion from the church were hushed up, but there were rumors that Niles had been experimenting with the occult.

"Soon after Niles moved back to Black Oaks, Angus went for a walk on the moors. When he didn't return, search parties were sent out." Loretta flashed a satanic grin. "They found his body. His throat had been torn out, and, according to a contemporaneous historical account, 'his face had a look of horror that haunted the dreams of all who looked upon him.'

"Niles McTavish took over Black Oaks as soon as his father was laid to rest, and the manor soon became the scene of—and I quote again—'debauched and drunken revels shunned by decent folk.' There were rumors that satanic rites were performed and orgies took place in the secret passageways and dungeon of the manor.

"Niles was denounced from the pulpit, but he had the local officials in his pocket, and nothing was done to curb his scandalous exploits. Given his reputation and the disgust with which he was viewed by the general public, you can imagine the dismay among the respectable elements of society when McTavish announced his betrothal to Alice Standish, the daughter of Ian Standish, Sexton's mayor. That 'Sweet Alice,' as she was called, would consent to marry Niles and that her father would not stand in the way of the match lent credence to the belief that witchcraft was involved. Of course, Ian might just have liked the idea of his daughter marrying a really rich guy."

"God, you're cynical," Robin said.

Loretta shrugged. "Law school trained me to look at both sides of an issue."

Robin laughed. "Continue."

"Okay. Well, two days of merrymaking preceded the wedding; read Spring Break Moors, with lots of drinking and lots of sex with devil worship thrown in for good measure.

"Niles had scheduled the wedding ceremony to take place at midnight. There's a legend that the Devil arrived at the stroke of twelve in a black coach drawn by seven coal-black horses and presented the groom with a carved wooden box engraved with a bloodred pentagram that contained a knife with a silver handle that looked like a claw that was half-human, half-wolf. The knife and the box actually existed. There were several witness accounts about that. But I couldn't find any cell phone shots of the Devil on Facebook or YouTube."

Robin laughed again. "I don't think you're taking this seriously."

Loretta smiled. "After midnight," she said, "the newlyweds retired to Niles's bedchamber. For days after, neither bride nor groom were seen. Meals were left outside the door, but, after the first day, they remained in the hall uneaten. A servant was always outside the door to receive orders. He reported hearing odd noises emanating from the room.

"When several days passed without Alice or Niles showing their faces, Alice's father demanded that Niles let him in. When he received no reply, he had the servants break down the door, and things got really weird."

"As if they weren't already," Robin interjected. Loretta's grin was positively ghoulish.

"Inside was a chamber of horrors. Alice was naked and dead. Her throat had been ripped apart, and her body was drenched in blood. Niles was nowhere to be found.

"Alice's father went insane when he saw his daughter's mangled body. He tore the room apart and found a false wall that opened into a passage that led to the moors. A search party was formed. The members claimed that they had not been able to find Niles, but days later a hunter found his mangled body. He had been sliced to ribbons, and the knife with the were-wolf handle was buried in his heart.

"Everyone suspected that Alice's father had done the deed, but every member of the search party swore that they had not found Niles. Ian lived in seclusion until he passed away a few years later."

"That's some story. What happened to Black Oaks?" Robin asked.

"Niles was the last of Angus McTavish's line, so there were no heirs. Given the bad vibes associated with Black Oaks, no one showed an interest in buying it or moving in, and the manor fell into disrepair. Over time, the village expanded and became a city, and the outer boundaries expanded until the city was less than a mile from Black Oaks. The Sexton Historical Society got a grant to restore it, and it became a museum and tourist attraction, which is how Katherine Melville, Nelly Melville's mother and Frank Melville's wife, discovered it.

"Katherine Melville inherited a vast family fortune that was made when logging was Oregon's main industry. She was obsessed with European history and became fascinated by the Black Oaks legend when she was studying at Oxford. When she got her inheritance, she decided to re-create Black Oaks in a remote area on Solitude Mountain. There are some modern additions, but most of the house on top of Solitude Mountain is a stone-by-stone re-creation of the original manor house in Sexton, England."

"What did you find out about Frank Melville?" Robin asked.

"There's a bit of a mystery here," Loretta said. "Melville was a DA in Multnomah County who specialized in prosecuting capital cases. After he left the DA's office, he joined Lawrence Trent's law firm. I talked with a friend at the firm. She told me that Melville was very successful, but a few years after going in with Trent he retired abruptly without giving a reason.

"Shortly after he retired, Frank and Katherine were in a terrible car accident. Katherine died, and Frank was paralyzed from the waist down. Melville has been living at Black Oaks since the accident, and he spends his time looking into the cases of convicted murderers who claim they're innocent. So far, his research has freed two men from prison.

"Frank and Katherine had one child, Nelly. She was inspired by her mother's passion and got a degree in European history at Columbia before going to Oxford to pursue a graduate degree. After the crash, she gave up her studies and moved to Black Oaks to take care of her father."

"I wonder why Melville quit practicing," Robin said.

"You can ask him, if you're still going to Black Oaks after hearing about the devil worship and supernatural animals."

"I'm more determined than ever now."

"Then I would advise you to bring a crucifix, holy water, and a necklace of garlic to the spooky castle."

Robin shook her head. "And here I thought you were

an ace researcher. The crucifix and that other stuff are for vampires. Werewolves can only be killed by silver bullets."

"My bad. So, you're going?"

"Only if there's no full moon tomorrow."

PART THREE

FRANK MELVILLE'S DILEMMA

CHAPTER SIX

During Oregon's rainy season, Oregonians, who were used to the whims of the weather gods, would ask if the mountains were out that day. On the morning of her journey to Black Oaks, the answer was definitely no. When Robin looked out her living room window, she saw thick black clouds floating over the river, hiding the mountains from view, and a bone-chilling rain that was dampening everyone's spirits, except Robin's. She was looking forward to her journey up Solitude Mountain to the cursed manor house.

Robin started the trip to Black Oaks in a downpour that ended almost as soon as she was on the road, and she continued her journey under an overcast sky. After a boring drive on a federal highway, she turned onto a state road that wound through farmland and orchards. As she drew closer to her destination, buildings grew scarcer, the space between them grew greater, the sky darkened, and rain began to fall again.

After a while, Robin found the turnoff to a narrow, poorly maintained, two-lane road that wound up the side of Solitude Mountain. Just before the junction, she passed the grounds of the hospital for the criminally insane. The complex had been built in the last century with bright red brick in this isolated setting on the theory that living in gaily colored buildings in the midst of a serene natural landscape would soothe the inmates.

While the people who'd built the mental hospital might have seen the surroundings as serene, Robin thought of them as desolate. In the years since the hospital opened, the brick had weathered to dull rust, the buildings and grounds had decayed, and the complex reminded Robin of Arkham Asylum from the Batman comics that she and her brothers read in middle school.

The original Black Oaks had been built near fog-enshrouded fens where quicksand could make a cow disappear in seconds and a man could easily lose his way. There were no moors on Solitude Mountain to make Robin feel uneasy, but being penned in between steep rock walls and a guardrail that was the only thing that protected her from hurtling over the abrupt edge of a cliff made Robin very nervous.

There were plenty of sharp curves on the mountain, and the downpour spattered on the windshield, making it hard to see the road. Robin had to slow down to navigate the hairpin turns. Even then, her car slipped on sections of the road where mud had slid onto the asphalt. Robin said a silent prayer of thanks to the technicians who had developed a braking system that was capable of keeping her on the straight and narrow.

It seemed like she'd been driving for hours when the road ended abruptly at an iron gate attached to a weathered stone wall. Robin phoned the house, but the call wouldn't go through. That's when she remembered Nelly had told her that cell phone reception was very bad on the mountain.

Nelly had mentioned a call box. Robin spotted one that was attached to the gate. Rain blew into the car when she lowered her window. There was a black button below a speaker. She pressed the button and heard static.

"This is Robin Lockwood," she said. "I'm at the front gate."

There was no response, and Robin started to worry. She pressed the button again and repeated herself. There was still no response, but, moments later, she heard a low hum, and the gate swung open.

A turn in a winding drive gave Robin her first view of Black Oaks. The manor was constructed of gray stone blocks turned darker by the constant assault of wind and rain. Several octagonal brick chimneys were scattered along an asymmetrical roofline that featured a turret here and a dormer there. Robin's overall impression was of a dwelling that had been slapped together without a coherent plan.

Robin parked, slung her canvas overnight bag over her shoulder, and ducked under the shelter provided by a portico that shielded an oversized wooden door from the elements. In the center of the door was an iron wolf's head knocker. Robin was about to use it when the door opened, and Robin had to use all of her self-control to keep from staring at the horrific scars that covered the left side of the face of the massive human being who filled the doorway.

"Welcome to Black Oaks, Miss Lockwood," the man said in a raspy voice that could have been the result of lung damage. "I'm Luther, Mr. Melville's houseman. May I help you with your bag?"

"I'm good," Robin said as she flashed a warm smile to show Luther that she wasn't put off by his deformity.

Luther stood back to let Robin into a cavernous entry hall where gray stone arches curved overhead to support a vaulted ceiling. A slender woman in a brown dress walked up to the houseman and laid a gentle hand on his forearm. Her face showed lines of age, and her gray hair was pulled back in a bun.

"Thank you, Luther. I'll take Miss Lockwood to her room."

Luther walked away, and the woman smiled at Robin.

"I'm Emily Raskin, Mr. Melville's housekeeper."

Mrs. Raskin led Robin down a gray stone hall decorated with tapestries showing medieval scenes. In one, men were hunting a wolf at night on the moors. Something about the wolf seemed off, but the light in the hall was dim. Robin remembered Loretta's jokes about a werewolf and Black Oaks, and she stopped to take a closer look.

She'd been right. There was something off about the wolf. It was standing on its hind legs, its front legs hanging down like a man's arms would, and it was looking over its shoulder toward the hunters with eyes more human than canine that stared from a face that was flatter and rounder than a wolf's and almost human in shape.

"Is that supposed to be a werewolf?" Robin asked Mrs. Raskin.

The housekeeper paused and turned. "So I've been told." She shook her head to show her disapproval. "I hate that thing. So does Mr. Melville. But he won't take it down because Mrs. Melville put it up."

"Was a similar tapestry in the original Black Oaks?"

"I wouldn't know. You'll have to ask Miss Nelly. Don't ask Mr. Melville. He believes in the Black Oaks curse and won't take kindly to your question."

"Thanks. I'll remember that."

Mrs. Raskin headed back down the hall at a brisk pace.

"This place is huge," Robin said. "How many people live at Black Oaks?"

"Mr. Melville, Miss Melville, and Miss Monroe live on the third floor in the east wing. The west wing is for guests. It's where you'll be staying.

"Luther and I have rooms on the second floor directly below the Melvilles'. No one lives in the other wing on the second floor."

The housekeeper stopped in front of a stone banister that ran along a staircase that curled toward the upper floors. The staircase was adjacent to a cage

elevator. The sides of the elevator car were made up
of narrowly spaced, black, wrought-iron bars decorated with gilded gold fleurettes.

Robin smiled. "I assume that this contraption
wasn't part of the original seventeenth-century manor
house."

"Miss Melville had this installed while her father
was recovering in the hospital," Mrs. Raskin explained
as she slid open the metal gate and stepped into a car
that was just big enough to accommodate a wheelchair
and two other passengers. Robin followed.

The buttons for the elevator were in a row from
top to bottom. Robin noticed that the buttons seemed
lower on the panel than the buttons in most elevators.
Mrs. Raskin saw where Robin was looking.

"Miss Melville had the buttons set lower than normal so Mr. Melville can reach them easily. The Stop/
Alarm button is even with Mr. Melville's eyes when
he's in his wheelchair so he can reach out and press it
if there's an emergency when he's in the car."

The button for the third floor was just under the
Stop/Alarm button. Mrs. Raskin pushed it in and re-
leased it, but the elevator didn't move. She looked at
Robin.

"Please slide the gate closed or the elevator won't
start."

Robin did as she was told, and the elevator rose
slowly. The car had just passed the second floor when
it jolted to an abrupt stop. Robin staggered backward
and regained her balance just as the car started again.

"Sorry," the housekeeper apologized. "The elevator does that between the second and third floor. I've kept after Mr. Melville to have it fixed, but he keeps putting it off. Someday the cables will snap, and the car will crash."

The housekeeper had made her prediction in a matter-of-fact tone, and Robin vowed to take the stairs from now on.

Robin and the housekeeper got out on the third floor, and Mrs. Raskin led Robin down a carpeted hall. She opened a door three doors down from the staircase revealing a spacious bedroom with a four-poster bed and a large oak armoire.

"You'll stay here, tonight. There's an intercom you can use if you want anything. I'll let Miss Nelly know you've arrived."

"Thanks, Mrs. Raskin."

As soon as the door closed behind the housekeeper, Robin walked over to a leaded glass window that looked out on the back of the estate. A flagstone patio separated the house from a lawn that ended at a sheer cliff. Robin knew that there was a valley beyond the cliff, but low-hanging clouds and sheets of rain hid it from view. A stiff wind was bowing the tops of the trees at the edge of the lawn. The sound it made reminded Robin of the call of a wolf, and she chided herself for having an overactive imagination.

Robin turned from the window and walked to the bed. She had worn a brown leather bomber jacket, jeans, and a sweater during the long ride. She opened her carry bag and laid a charcoal-gray business suit and white satin blouse on the bed before going into the bathroom.

Robin had just washed up and changed when there was a knock on her door. An attractive woman in her midthirties wearing jeans and a sky-blue, cable-knit sweater was standing in the hall. Her light red hair was cut short. She had green eyes, a turned-up nose, and a pale, freckled face. The woman was holding a tray with a sandwich and a cup of coffee, and she smiled at Robin.

"I'm Nelly Melville, Miss Lockwood. I thought you might like something to eat before you meet my father."

"Please call me Robin, and that sandwich looks great."

Nelly set down the tray on a table by the window, and Robin attacked the sandwich.

"How was your trip?" Nelly asked.

"Long, and I was scared to death driving up the mountain."

Nelly laughed. "I doubt that someone who fought professionally would be scared of anything."

Robin smiled. "So, you've been checking up on me."

"Of course. You aren't the only lawyer Dad asked me to vet, but you were certainly the most interesting. How did you fight on TV and go to law school at the same time? It sounds impossible."

"The workload in law school did make it hard to

train and spend time away in Vegas for the fights. Fortunately, I didn't do both for long."

"Oh, what happened?"

"During my first semester at Yale, there was a big pay-per-view card in Vegas. Mandy Kerrigan was supposed to fight Angelina Mendes in the co-main event. The winner was going to fight for the championship. Then, shortly before the fight, Mendes broke her ankle. Kerrigan was the number-two contender. I was ranked ninth in the weight class and I was on the card, so I was training. They asked me to step in so they wouldn't have to cancel the fight. I was really excited, but my manager didn't want me to go into the cage with Mandy. I wouldn't listen."

Robin smiled when she remembered what had happened once the bell rang.

"Kerrigan was way out of my league. She knocked me out in the first round and knocked some sense into me. I had a concussion and short-term memory loss, and I decided it was a lot less painful arguing with a professor who could beat your head in intellectually but wasn't allowed to kick you in the head for real."

Nelly laughed.

"Did you like studying at Oxford?" Robin asked.

"So, you checked me out too?"

"You'd think less of me if I hadn't." Robin smiled. "I also checked out the history of Black Oaks with its werewolves and the spooky curse."

Nelly's countenance darkened. "Please don't make fun of the curse when you're with Dad. He believes it, and I can't blame him. Nothing good has happened since my parents moved into this monstrosity. First, Dad quit his law practice for no apparent reason. Then there was the accident . . ."

"Do you have any idea why your father retired so abruptly?"

Nelly shook her head. "He refuses to talk about it."

"If your father thinks Black Oaks is cursed, why does he stay here?"

"I've begged him to leave, but my mother loved the place. Dad says he can sense her presence in every room, and he'd feel like he was deserting her if he left."

Robin understood exactly how Frank Melville felt. She'd sensed Jeff's presence in every room of the apartment she and Jeff shared, but she'd decided that the pain of staying with those constant reminders was too great. She'd also believed that Jeff would live in her heart no matter where she stayed.

"So, did you enjoy Oxford?" Robin asked, hoping that a change of subject would lighten the mood. It didn't.

"I wasn't there long enough to know," Nelly said. "Dad had his accident my third week at the university, and I flew home."

"Sorry."

"Don't be. I love my father and I've never regretted being here for him."

"Have you learned why he wants to see me?"

"He won't discuss that either. But you'll know soon enough. He's waiting to meet you."

* * *

The top of the stone staircase divided the third floor into two wings. Guests were housed in several rooms adjacent to the one Robin occupied in the west wing, and the Melville family occupied the rooms in the east wing. Robin followed Nelly Melville to the end of the third-floor corridor. Nelly knocked on the last door, and a deep voice told her to enter.

Frank Melville's suite took up the entire end of the manor. The room Robin walked into was dominated by an ornately carved desk with a kneehole wide enough to accommodate Melville's wheelchair.

Melville's deep voice had tricked Robin into expecting her host to be robust, but Frank Melville was a man weighed down by sorrow. His thin skin was pale, and his hair was gray with a sprinkling of strands that were the same cinnamon color as his daughter's tresses. His green eyes looked tired.

Melville was wearing a tweed jacket, white shirt, and navy blue tie. Across from him was a tall woman with shoulder-length, honey-blond hair and sky-blue eyes, who looked closer to Nelly's age than her father's.

"Thank you for coming all this way, Miss Lockwood," Melville said. "I hope the trip wasn't too arduous."

"I survived it in one piece," Robin answered with a smile.

"Well, you're here now, and I appreciate it."

Melville gestured toward the woman seated across from him.

"This is Sheila Monroe, my assistant, without whom

I could never have done my work to free the innocent from prison."

Robin could feel the warmth that flowed toward the woman. But she also noticed that Nelly had tensed up.

"Sheila and Nelly, I'd like you to leave. I know you're curious about why I asked Miss Lockwood to come to Black Oaks, but it's a legal matter, and I'm sure you appreciate that many of the things I am going to relate will constitute a confidential communication."

"Of course, Frank," Sheila said as she stood to leave.

"I'll see you at dinner," Nelly said as she left the room.

Melville told Robin to take the seat that Sheila Monroe had vacated. As soon as they were alone, his shoulders sagged, and he looked desperate.

"Miss Lockwood, I need your help to right a terrible wrong." Melville took a deep breath and gathered himself. "It's going to take some time for me to explain what happened."

"Take all the time you need, and give me as much information as you can, so I can figure out how to help."

Melville looked down at the desktop. Robin could see that he was in distress.

"I started my legal career in the Multnomah County district attorney's office. I was an excellent prosecutor with an almost perfect record of convictions. Within a relatively short time, I was the lead prosecutor in the section that handled capital cases. Most of the men and women I prosecuted ended up on death row, and I never regretted exacting justice for the victims of heinous crimes."

Melville took another deep breath. "Thirty years ago, I prosecuted Jose Alvarez for the murder of Margo Prescott. They were students at Randolph College who met because they were rock climbing enthusiasts. She was premed, and he was studying engineering, and they were in the early stages of a relationship. On the evening of the murder, several witnesses saw the couple have a heated argument. Around ten o'clock, Prescott's roommate returned from a date and found Margo Prescott bludgeoned to death.

"The police canvassed for witnesses. Archie Stallings, another Randolph student, testified at Alvarez's trial that he was passing Prescott's dorm around nine when he saw Jose run out. He thought there was blood on his shirt.

"The police questioned Jose. He said that he and Prescott had argued because she wanted to break up with him. He was certain that she was being pressured by her family, who are wealthy, because she was dating a poor son of Mexican immigrants. He admitted that he had run out of Prescott's dorm around nine, but he denied killing Prescott. He said that he wanted to talk to her and found her dead.

"The detectives asked Jose why he hadn't called them. He said that he had grown up in a neighborhood where the police were seen as enemies, and he was afraid he would not be believed because he was Mexican.

"The crime lab found a bloody handprint on Prescott's body and linked it to Jose. The lab also determined that one of Alvarez's shirts had Prescott's blood on it. Jose said he was in shock when he saw Margo's body. He tried to revive her and got her blood on his shirt. The detectives were convinced that Alvarez was guilty. They arrested him, and he was charged with aggravated murder.

"I was also convinced that Jose was guilty, but I offered him a plea deal because he had never had any problems with the police before and was a model student. He refused the offer and went to trial. I didn't think Jose's public defender was very well prepared, but the trial was clean with no appellate issues.

"The key witness in the case was Archie Stallings, the charming son of affluent parents. He was a great witness. A jury found Jose guilty, and he was sentenced to death. There have been multiple appeals in state and federal court, and there was a moratorium on death sentences for several years, so Jose is still alive."

Melville took another deep breath, and Robin could see that talking about the case was an ordeal.

"A year or so after the Alvarez case, I left the DA's office and went into private practice with Lawrence Trent. I'd known Larry since high school, and I enjoyed working with him and the other people in the firm. I found that I had a knack for personal injury work, and I did quite well. I also took on the occasional criminal case. One of the people who hired me was Archie Stallings, who had been charged with rape."

Melville paused, and Robin suddenly saw where this was going. When her host continued, he looked sick.

"The police interviewed several women who testified that Stallings had tried to force himself on them. Some of these incidents happened after Margo Prescott was murdered. But two happened before she was killed. More important, one witness, Debra Porter, said she was a friend of Margo Prescott and that Margo had told her that Stallings had come on to her at a party and had tried to force her into a bedroom, but was prevented when another student intervened. That student was Jose Alvarez. None of this came out at Jose's trial.

"I won a motion on Stallings's behalf to keep out the testimony of the women. Then I won Stallings's trial. After the acquittal, Stallings and I went back to my office, where he confessed that he had killed Prescott and that Alvarez was completely innocent.

"Stallings said he had met Prescott outside her dorm. She was upset because she had broken up with Jose. Stallings pretended to be sympathetic, and they went to her room so she could vent. When they were in Prescott's room, Stallings tried to get her into bed. When she resisted, he hit her. She threatened to tell the police, and he panicked and beat her to death so she couldn't incriminate him.

"Stallings told me that he left Prescott's room just as Jose was coming up the stairs. He hid until Jose was in Prescott's room. Then he left the dorm and waited to see what would happen after Jose discovered the body. When he saw Jose run out of the dorm, he called nine-one-one anonymously. Stallings told me that he incriminated Alvarez because he was jealous that Prescott was having sex with a Mexican, but had rejected him.

"As you know, the attorney-client privilege made it impossible for me to tell anyone what Stallings had told me in confidence without his consent. I begged him to let me tell the authorities that Jose was innocent, but he told me he'd have me disbarred if I did, and he'd deny ever telling me that he'd killed Prescott. I was consumed by guilt. I became depressed and retired. I just couldn't practice law anymore."

Tears welled up. Melville tried to compose himself and failed.

"The accident . . . It happened soon after . . ."

Melville took a deep breath, and Robin waited patiently.

"There is a curse on anyone who lives in Black Oaks, and God visited that curse on me when he took my Katherine away and left me like this. To atone for letting Jose Alvarez rot in prison while I knew he was innocent, I've tried to save other innocent defendants, but even my few victories haven't brought me peace. Then I learned that Stallings had died from a heart attack, and I decided to try and save Jose. That's why I brought you here. I want you to do what I can't. I want you to save Jose's life."

When their meeting ended, Frank Melville gave Robin two large suitcases. One was filled with a copy of the files from the Alvarez case and a confidential memo detailing everything Melville knew about it. The other suitcase contained the multivolume transcript of the trial.

Robin rolled the suitcases to her room and started reading the case file. She was partway through the police reports when there was a knock on her door. Robin put down the report she was reading and said, "Come in."

Sheila Monroe opened the door.

"I've been sent to escort you to dinner," she said, flashing a warm smile.

"Thanks. All I had to eat was a sandwich Nelly brought me, and I'm famished."

Sheila's smile disappeared. Robin was certain that Monroe had something on her mind and was trying to decide whether to tell her what it was.

"I know you're not supposed to talk about the reason Frank sent for you, but does it concern the Alvarez case?" Monroe asked.

"I can't answer that question."

Sheila nodded. "I understand. But if that's why you're here, you've got to help him. He's never told me what happened, but he's obsessed with Alvarez."

Monroe paused again. Robin waited for her to continue.

"You know I'm Frank's research assistant?" she said after a pause.

"Yes."

"Soon after he hired me, he had me do exhaustive research on the attorney-client privilege and a deep dig into Archie Stallings's life. I know Stallings was the key witness in the Alvarez case, and I'm certain that he told Frank something that convinced Frank that Alvarez is innocent. But he clams up any time I raise the subject."

Sheila's shoulders were hunched from tension, and her hands had curled into fists.

"That case is tearing Frank apart. If that's why you're here, please help him."

Robin flashed Melville's assistant a reassuring smile.

"You can count on me to try to bring the task Mr. Melville set for me to a successful conclusion."

Monroe's shoulders relaxed, her hands uncurled, and she looked relieved. "Thank you. Now let's go down to dinner."

Sheila escorted Robin to a cavernous dining hall paneled in dark wood and lighted by several chandeliers. During the day, the room was illuminated by sunlight that flowed through a set of stained-glass windows decorated with biblical themes that would have been at home in a European cathedral. At one end of the room was a massive stone fireplace where a fire provided enough heat to counteract the chill from the wind that whipped around the outside of the manor house and slipped through cracks in the stone walls.

Robin, Nelly, Sheila Monroe, and Frank Melville ate dinner at one end of a long table that could have easily accommodated sixteen more guests. It was obvious that Nelly wanted to know what Frank and Robin had discussed, but she was too polite to ask. Robin diverted her attention with stories about her experiences as a cage fighter and gossip about the celebrities she'd met.

After dinner, Robin went back to her room. She wasn't tired, so she decided to continue looking at the Alvarez file. She closed the door and wandered over to the window before going to her bed where she'd spread out the police reports. Clouds blocked whatever moonlight might have shone down on the estate, but a little ambient light from a few windows let her see trees swaying in the wind from the storm that still raged outside.

Robin started to turn from the window, but she stopped halfway. When she was very small, there had been a brief time when she wouldn't go to sleep without a night-light because of a feeling of dread that possessed her when her room turned dark. She had been certain that some unnamed thing materialized in her closet or under her bed or in the corner of her room when the light disappeared.

The wind was making the howling sound she'd heard before. It was muffled by the thick stone walls of the manor house, but, for a moment, Robin thought the pitch changed, and that nameless dread from her childhood filled her. Was she hearing the wind or the howling of a wolf?

"Damn Loretta," Robin swore. All that stuff about werewolves had primed her to misinterpret the sound.

It was definitely the wind, she told herself. There were no wolves on Solitude Mountain and no werewolves anywhere.

Robin returned to the Alvarez case file and continued reading until her eyes grew heavy. She had made notes while she was reading, and she had jotted down two legal issues that needed to be researched.

It was only ten, and she thought Loretta would still be up. Robin got out her cell phone, but there were no bars. She looked around the room for a phone. When she didn't see one, she pressed the button on the intercom.

"Mrs. Raskin," she said when the housekeeper answered, "I have to call my associate in Portland, but I'm not getting any cell service. Is there a landline I could use?"

"There's a phone in the library," Mrs. Raskin answered. "Do you know where that is?"

"No."

"Walk down to the first floor. It's next to the dining room."

"Thanks."

Robin walked into the hall. The elevator was waiting on the third floor, but Robin remembered how certain Mrs. Raskin had been about the inevitability of the car crashing, so she opted for the stairs.

It was eerily quiet in the great house, but that wasn't surprising with only a handful of residents in a mansion that could double as a hotel. The lighting on the first floor was very dim, and there were shadows everywhere; shadows that could conceal anything. Robin shivered. Then she slapped her cheek.

"Man up," she chided herself before making a mental note to sue Loretta for emotional distress.

The library was a small room dominated by floor-to-ceiling shelves filled with books, many of which appeared to have been read. At the far end of the room was a fireplace with a carved wooden mantel. There was no fire in the fireplace, and the room was very cold. Armchairs stood on either side of the fireplace, and an end table stood beside each chair. There was a phone on one of the end tables.

Robin sat down and dialed Loretta's cell phone. Her associate picked up on the second ring.

"Did I wake you?" Robin asked.

"Nah. I'm binge-watching a really cool thriller on Netflix."

"Pause it. I've got a few things I need you to research. Do you have a pen?"

"Give me a sec."

When Loretta got back on the phone, Robin gave her a rough outline of what Frank Melville had told her about Jose Alvarez's case.

"I'll be back late tomorrow afternoon," Robin said. "I need to know if we raise our issues in state or federal court and any ideas you have for getting past the attorney-client privilege."

"Got it. So, seen any werewolves yet?"

Robin laughed. "Remind me to fire you when I get back. Black Oaks is the creepiest place I've ever been, and all that scary stuff you told me about devil worship and werewolves has made me a nervous wreck."

"Will I get a nice severance package?"

"Absolutely not. And don't expect a good letter of recommendation."

Loretta laughed. "See you tomorrow, boss."

"See you then."

CHAPTER SEVEN

Robin went to bed a little before midnight and was awakened by sunlight. She stretched and walked to the window. The storm had passed, and the scene that greeted her was completely different from the eerie landscape that helped to form Robin's first impression of Black Oaks.

Colorful flower beds and a variety of emerald-green shrubs decorated a green lawn that stretched from a flagstone patio to the forest that set the boundaries of the estate. Looming over the forest was the snow-covered peak of one of the Cascade mountains.

Robin packed before going downstairs for breakfast. Mrs. Raskin greeted her at the entrance to the dining room and asked her what she wanted to eat. Robin anticipated a long trip back to Portland and asked if she could get eggs and hash browns.

"Would you like bacon, sausage, or biscuits with your eggs?" Mrs. Raskin asked.

Robin laughed. "Bacon and a biscuit would be fabulous."

"If you give me your keys, I'll have Luther bring your bags to your car."

Robin gave her the keys to her car and walked into the dining room. Nelly Melville was seated at one end of the dining table. Robin took a seat next to her.

"I can't thank you enough for coming to Black Oaks," Nelly said. "I don't know why Dad wanted to talk to you, but he was so upbeat this morning. Whatever you told him has made him happier than I've seen him in years."

At that moment, Sheila Monroe followed Frank Melville's wheelchair into the dining room. Melville flashed a wide smile when he saw Robin.

"I'm so glad you haven't left. I was worried I'd miss you."

"Mrs. Raskin is preparing a feast for me, so I won't starve on the trip to Portland."

"Have you had a chance to go over the file I gave you?"

"I made a little headway last night."

"And?"

"My associate is researching the key issues. I'll be able to give you a better opinion of our chances when I talk to her."

Robin's experience on the return trip down Solitude Mountain was as different from the journey up as the view had been this morning from her first sight of the mansion. During the ride up, a pounding rain and the rapid sweep of the wiper blades had made every inch she had traveled an adventure. During the trip back, she found it easy to handle the curves, although she did have to concentrate when she was forced to maneuver around mud that covered parts of the road. Robin wondered if serious mudslides or avalanches of rock and dirt ever blocked the road and cut off Black Oaks from the outside world.

Robin experienced a feeling of relief when she saw the grounds of the state hospital and knew that her journey down the mountain was over. And it was then, when she stopped having to concentrate on the road down the mountain and began thinking about the Alvarez case again, that it occurred to her that she hadn't thought about Jeff Hodges since she'd left for Black Oaks, the previous morning.

The thought unsettled her for a moment. Was she glad that Black Oaks had distracted her from the pain she experienced every time thoughts of Jeff intruded? No, but she appreciated being freed from the pain caused by memories of what she had lost.

Robin smiled. She had loved Jeff, and still loved him as much as she had while he was alive. She resolved to keep thinking about their good times and not dwell on her loss. She knew that wouldn't be easy, but it would be worth the effort if she could find peace.

Robin walked into the waiting room of Barrister, Berman, and Lockwood at three o'clock. After asking her secretary if there were any emergencies and checking her emails, Robin told Loretta and Ken Breland, the firm's investigator, to meet her in the conference room.

When Robin walked in, her investigator and her associate were seated on one side of a long conference table. Robin dumped the transcripts and files in the center of the table and sat across from them. Then she handed Ken and Loretta a copy of Melville's memo.

Robin turned to her investigator, an ex–Navy SEAL, who had worked as a spy before retiring from government work. Ken was slender, clean-cut, and five foot ten with a full head of short, silver hair, and he looked more like a CPA than someone who had been a spook for the CIA.

"How much do you know about my trip to Black Oaks?"

"Only what Loretta told me."

"We've been hired by Frank Melville to save an innocent man who's on death row. You'll need to go through this stuff," Robin said, pointing at the center of the conference table. "We can talk when you're up to speed."

Robin turned to Loretta. "What have you got for me?"

"Getting Stallings's confession in may be a problem. The attorney-client privilege is still in effect even if the client dies. If Melville can't tell the judge that Stallings confessed, we're dead in the water."

"Any ideas about how we can circumvent that problem?"

"I have some ideas, but I haven't had time to see if they'll work."

"Any other problems?"

"Well, yeah. Even if Melville can tell a court about Stallings's confession, we'll still have to corroborate it with evidence, like the testimony of that woman who knew about Prescott and Stallings."

"That's going to be your job," Robin told Ken.

Breland nodded.

"Any other problems?"

"A big one. The statute of limitations has run out on raising Alvarez's post-conviction issues in our state courts."

"What about federal habeas corpus?" Robin asked.

"I'm looking into that avenue."

"Okay. That's enough for now." Robin pointed to the center of the table. "We'll all have to read through the files and trial transcripts. When you do, keep one thought in your mind. This case doesn't involve reasonable doubt or some violation of an evidence rule or a provision of the constitution. Jose Alvarez is on death row. We now know he is completely innocent, and he will die if we don't do our job."

After the meeting broke up, Robin grabbed several trial transcripts and took them into her office. The long ride back to Portland from Black Oaks had tired her, and she stopped reading when the words began swimming on the page. Robin stuffed two volumes of the trial transcripts in a book bag, bought a rainbow roll and an unagi avocado roll at her favorite sushi restaurant, and headed to her condo.

Robin's first job in Oregon had been a clerkship at

the Oregon Supreme Court in Salem. When Regina Barrister hired her as an associate, she drove up I-5 and moved into a small apartment in a trendy area of Portland on the east side of the Willamette River that was known for its restaurants and locally owned shops. Jeff Hodges had moved in soon after they started dating, and they were living there when he died. Robin tried to stay in their apartment after Jeff's death, but the place was filled with ghosts.

Now Robin lived in a modern, high-rise condo on the west side of the river with a view of snowcapped mountains and the Willamette that was a fifteen-minute walk from her office. Robin treasured the view because it was so different from the view she and Jeff had shared and didn't evoke memories that made her sad.

Robin waved at the security guard and took the elevator to her floor. The neighbors in her old apartment house had been artists, students, or new professionals, and they tended to be friendly. Her new neighbors worked long hours. They were partners in prestigious law and accounting firms and successful businessmen and -women. Robin rarely saw them, but that was okay, because she wasn't interested in socializing.

As soon as she was inside, Robin changed into sweats and ate her dinner. Then she took out the transcripts but didn't have the energy to read for long. There was a UFC fight on TV. She knew some of the fighters from her MMA days and tuned in to see how they did, but she only lasted through a few bouts before she switched off the set and dragged herself into the bed-room. It was early, but that was okay. She wanted to get a good night's sleep because she would be starting a quest to save Jose Alvarez's life when the sun rose.

PART FOUR

HABEAS CORPUS

CHAPTER EIGHT

In order to find Debra Porter, Ken Breland did not have to call in a favor from an old friend at the CIA or hack into the files of the NSA. He just had to log into Facebook, where he found many pictures of the Randolph College alum, including one of her outside the high school where she had been an English teacher for twenty years.

Ken studied Porter's photo while he waited next to her car in the teachers' parking lot outside Ida B. Wells High School. He knew which car was Porter's because he'd gotten the number of her plate from a friend at the Department of Motor Vehicles. Half an hour after class had been dismissed, a heavyset woman in her fifties walked toward him.

"Mrs. Porter?" Ken asked when Debra approached her parking space.

"Yes."

Ken handed Debra his card. "I wonder if you could

spare a few minutes to talk about a case I'm working on for Robin Lockwood."

"The attorney?"

"Yes, ma'am."

Flashing his employer's name usually got Ken's foot in the door. A lot of Robin's cases had been front-page news, and the media loved the fact that she was attractive and lethal.

Debra looked confused. "What kind of case are you talking about?"

"One that involves your days as a student at Randolph College."

Debra's mouth gaped open. "You're not talking about Margo?"

"Yes, ma'am, and Jose Alvarez. We have new information that suggests he may be innocent. I noticed that there's a coffee shop near here. I'd be glad to spring for a latte while we talk about it."

Debra Porter eyed Ken with suspicion as he approached with her drink.

"One caramel macchiato," Ken said as he sat across from her.

"You still haven't told me what you want," Debra said.

"Do you remember a student named Archie Stallings?" Ken said as he pried the plastic lid off his black coffee.

Debra flushed with anger. "That man is a pig."

"Was a pig," Ken corrected. "He died recently."

"Good riddance."

"That's some reaction, care to explain it?"

"Why don't you tell me why you think Jose Alvarez is innocent before I answer any more questions, because the last I heard, he'd been convicted of beating Margo to death."

"Archie Stallings's testimony for the prosecution was a major reason for the conviction. Miss Lockwood has come into possession of evidence that calls his testimony into question."

"In what way?"

"For various legal reasons, I'm barred from telling you what Miss Lockwood learned. I can ask you if you have any reason to believe that Stallings may have lied at Jose's trial?"

Debra took a sip of her drink and stared into space. Ken let her think. After a moment, she looked at Ken.

"A detective talked to me when Stallings was charged with rape. I told her that there were rumors that he'd been aggressive with more than one girl. I also told her that Margo had told me that he'd come on to her at a party, and Jose had stopped him from forcing her into a bedroom."

"Were you and Margo good friends? Someone she would confide in?"

"Yes, and she told me Archie had been after her and wouldn't take no for an answer."

"Why didn't you testify about that at Jose's trial?"

"No one asked me, so I thought it wasn't important. But I've always wondered . . ." Debra paused. "If I'd told someone when Jose was on trial, would it have helped?"

"Possibly."

Debra looked down. "I feel terrible."

"Don't. Jose's attorney should have found you. It was his responsibility. And you may have a chance now to right a terrible wrong."

CHAPTER NINE

The firm's receptionist buzzed Ken Breland as soon as Robin arrived at Barrister, Berman, and Lockwood fresh from her workout. Ken met Robin halfway and walked down the hall with her toward her office.

"I've some really good stuff for you," Breland said.

Robin held her office door open for Ken. "Let's talk."

It was rainy and cold outside, and Robin was wearing a fleece-lined parka. She hung it up and took a seat behind her desk while Ken took one of her client chairs.

"So?" Robin said as she peeled the plastic lid off her latte and took a sip.

"If you need to show that Jose's attorney was incompetent or that Archie Stallings is a creep who molests women, we're in fat city."

At five the previous evening, Loretta had briefed Robin on her theory of how to breach the barrier erected by the attorney-client confidence. When she left the office, Robin had been hopeful about her chances in Jose's case. She was in a great mood when Ken finished his report.

As soon as she was alone, Robin phoned Black Oaks.

"Good morning, Mr. Melville," Robin said when her client came on the line.

"Do you have news for me?"

"I do. My investigator talked to three of the women whose testimony you suppressed, and they're all willing to testify that Stallings was a sexual predator. More important, one of them, Debra Porter, will testify that Stallings tried to force Margo Prescott into a bedroom at a party, and Jose stopped him. So, Stallings had a reason to perjure himself at Jose's trial, and Jose's lawyer should have called these women so the jury would know that Stallings had a reason to lie about Jose."

"What about getting my testimony before a judge? Have you found a way around the attorney-client privilege?"

"I think so. It will be a close call, but my associate came up with an idea I think might work."

"Will you have a problem with the statute of limitations?"

"We're barred in state court, but we can go into federal court. I'm going to argue that Jose was denied his Sixth Amendment right to counsel. We'll allege that his trial lawyer was incompetent because he didn't find the women who could have impeached Stallings. I'm also going to argue that Jose is completely innocent. That's another ground for granting habeas corpus that the Feds recognize."

"It sounds like you're on the right track. What's your next move?"

"I didn't want to get Jose's hopes up before I thought I could help him, so I haven't met with him to tell him that we're going to reopen his case. Now that I think we have a good shot at getting him out, I'm going to drive down to the penitentiary and introduce myself."

"That's wonderful. Please let me know what happens when you meet Jose."

"I'll call you as soon as I get back to my office."

As soon as the call ended, Frank Melville leaned his head against the back of his wheelchair and closed his eyes. Robin Lockwood had seemed so positive on the phone. Could his nightmare finally be over? Was it possible that he was going to be absolved of the guilt that had sickened him ever since Archie Stallings had confessed and he'd lacked the courage to tell the truth?

Melville had convinced himself that nothing would have been gained if he'd told the authorities that Stallings had murdered Margo Prescott. Stallings would have said that he never confessed, and Frank would have had no way to disprove the lie. And there was a good chance that he would have been censured or disbarred for revealing an attorney-client confidence. Melville would have risked losing his career if it resulted in freeing Jose Alvarez from the cage into which he had put the young man, but his efforts would have been futile while Stallings was still alive. Now that Stallings was dead, there was hope for Jose and a chance that he could be at peace after years of self-condemnation. If Robin did succeed, Melville vowed that he would do everything in his power to make amends to Jose Alvarez for the life that had been stolen from him.

It occurred to Frank that there was a chance that he would actually be happy if Robin succeeded. And there was something else that might happen if Robin won. Something he didn't dare do unless Jose was a free man.

After Katherine died Frank resigned himself to a life of loneliness. He couldn't imagine meeting anyone whom he could love like he'd loved Katherine or who could love a cripple. Then Sheila Monroe had come into his life. He had never revealed his feelings to her. More important, while she was kind and supportive, she had never given him any indication that she had strong feelings for him.

Frank could not bring himself to tell Sheila how he felt while Jose languished in prison. But if Robin succeeded in clearing Jose's name . . .

Frank took a deep breath. Best not to dream of what might be. Not after so many of his dreams had been turned to dust. Best to wait and see what happened when Robin went to court.

CHAPTER TEN

Robin parked in the visitors' lot of the Oregon State Penitentiary and walked down a tree-lined lane toward the squat, square prison with its thick, egg-yolk-yellow walls, barbed-wire fences, and gun towers. A short flight of stairs led to a door that opened into a waiting room lined with couches covered in rust-colored upholstery that had been manufactured in the prison.

A young woman had just gotten up from one of the couches and was trying to keep a toddler from running away from her. She looked exhausted and angry. Robin wondered if she was here to visit the boy's father. How far did she have to travel, how often did she visit? The child's clothes looked like hand-me-downs, and her clothes looked frayed. Robin wondered what life had in store for the little boy.

Two guards were stationed behind a circular counter in the center of the room. Robin showed them her photo ID and bar card and told them the purpose of her visit. One of the guards walked around the desk and led Robin to a metal detector. After she walked through it, he escorted her down a ramp, through two sets of sliding steel bars, and down a short hall. Robin waited while the guard unlocked the thick metal door that opened into the visiting area, a large, open space furnished with vending machines that dispensed drinks and snacks. The prisoners were easy to identify in their blue jeans and work shirts. They sat on prison-made couches and talked in low tones to their parents, wives or girlfriends, or played with children they got to see once a month.

Robin walked up to a corrections officer who sat on a raised platform at one end of the room.

"I'm Robin Lockwood. I'm an attorney, and I'd like to talk to Jose Alvarez. He's one of the inmates on death row."

"They called me when you checked in at the front desk. Mr. Alvarez will be down in about fifteen minutes."

The guard got down from the platform. "You can talk to Mr. Alvarez in the first noncontact visiting room. It's at the end of the hall across the way. Follow me."

The guard led Robin to another open area lined on two walls with bulletproof glass windows where attorneys could talk to prisoners who were deemed to be too dangerous to be allowed in the visiting room. At the end of this area were the two tiny rooms where death row inmates could meet with their attorneys. The guard escorted Robin to one of them and ushered her inside. A bridge chair faced a glass window set in concrete blocks painted institutional brown. A slot for passing papers was set in the bottom of the window, and a metal ledge just wide enough to accommodate a legal pad jutted out of the wall beneath the window. A phone receiver was attached to the wall. On the other side of the glass was a room that was a mirror image of the one Robin was in.

After twenty minutes passed, a door opened and Alvarez walked in. Fighters have to make weight, and they get good at estimating it. Robin saw a welterweight in the 147-pound range; slender, muscular, and in better shape than she would have expected given the starchy food prisoners were served and the limited amount of exercise someone on death row would get. Alvarez's black hair had streaks of gray, and his brown eyes were a shade darker than his skin.

The prisoner sat down on a folding chair on the other side of the glass. Robin picked up her receiver. Jose stared at her. She motioned toward the receiver on his side. Alvarez picked it up. He looked suspicious and tense.

"Who are you?" he demanded.

"My name is Robin Lockwood, and I'm an attorney."

"Why are you here? I don't know you."

"I'm here to help you. I know for a fact that you didn't kill Margo Prescott, and I've been hired to get your conviction reversed."

"Who hired you? I don't know anyone who would want to help me."

"This must be very confusing. Let me explain. I have a law firm in Portland, and I specialize in criminal defense. A few weeks ago, I was hired by Frank Melville, the district attorney who prosecuted you. When he tried your case, he was convinced that you murdered Margo Prescott. Then, he came into possession of evidence that convinced him that he'd made a terrible mistake and that you are completely innocent."

"What evidence?"

"A person he was representing confessed to the murder."

Jose looked stunned. "When did he get this evidence?"

"Several years ago."

"And he waited until now to try and get me out!" Alvarez said, suddenly furious.

"I can understand how angry you must be, but there's a reason Mr. Melville couldn't act sooner. The evidence was in the form of a confidence told to him by a client, which he was forbidden by law to disclose because of the attorney-client privilege. The man who confessed told Mr. Melville that he couldn't tell anyone you were innocent. He said that he would deny his confession if Mr. Melville went public, and there were no witnesses to the conversation who could back up Mr. Melville. The person who confessed to killing Margo Prescott died recently, and Mr. Melville hired me to see if I could free you from death row."

Alvarez looked down at the narrow metal ledge where a prisoner could rest papers. Robin could see that he was barely able to contain his anger.

"I've been rotting here for thirty years. Thirty years! Do you understand what that's like? Caged like an animal and treated like one, when Melville knew that I was innocent?"

"I know it won't make you feel better to learn that Mr. Melville was so overwhelmed by guilt that he stopped practicing law."

"You're damn right it doesn't."

"And I would never tell you that I can understand how horrible this has been for you. I can just promise that I will do everything in my power to end your ordeal."

Alvarez looked up and laughed without a trace of humor.

"*Ordeal.* That's a lawyer word. A pretty vocabulary choice that can't even begin to describe how every minute of every day has been torture."

"You're right. I apologize. As I said, I won't pretend that I'll ever be able to understand what you've gone through. I will tell you that I'm convinced that we have the ammunition to get your case overturned, and I promise you that I will do everything in my power to get you out of the cage you're in."

"What exactly do you plan to do?" Alvarez demanded.

Robin pushed several documents to Alvarez through the paper pass.

"These are pleadings I've prepared and several legal memos I'm going to file. I plan to challenge your conviction in federal court on the grounds that your trial attorney was incompetent. We've found several witnesses who will swear that the person who really killed Margo Prescott was a sexual predator who had propositioned Miss Prescott for sex."

"Are you talking about Archie Stallings?"

Robin looked down, unable to meet Jose's eye.

"I'm afraid I can't answer your question."

"Why not?"

"I received the information in confidence from Mr. Melville. I'm his agent, and I'm bound by the same rule of evidence that kept Mr. Melville from revealing what his client told him in confidence."

Jose laughed, but there was no humor in it. "More lawyer bullshit, mumbo jumbo."

Alvarez stood up, turned his back on Robin.

"Please, Mr. Alvarez."

Alvarez rang for the guard. "I'm done here," he said.

Robin never expected Jose to thank her, and she was not insulted. Thirty years was a long time to experience despair and to have anger eating away at you.

The guard opened the door, and Jose disappeared behind it. Robin didn't move. She stared through the glass, wondering what kind of life Jose Alvarez would lead if she won.

The bars slammed shut on the tiny cell that had been Jose Alvarez's home for thirty years. He stood in the center of the floor and stared at the wall, but he didn't see the stark gray concrete. All he saw were the wasted years; the years that had been stolen from him.

Rage tightened every muscle in his body until it felt like tendons would rip and his bones would shatter.

Jose's fingers curled into fists, and he smashed them into the wall until his knuckles bled. Then he threw himself onto the floor and did push-up after push-up. When his biceps turned to putty, he collapsed on the cold concrete and sobbed.

Frank Melville had put him in this coffin. Frank Melville could have gotten him out and did not. Frank Melville had robbed him of his future, a family, children, a *life*!

Until now, Jose had hated the world, but now his hate was focused on one man.

CHAPTER ELEVEN

Jose Alvarez had gotten lucky. It wasn't unusual for attorneys on both sides to ask for continuances when a defendant alleges that he is being held illegally, but Jose's case had moved more quickly than most, and, two months after filing for relief, the parties were ready for trial.

During those two months, Robin had handled several other cases while Ken Breland obtained notarized affidavits from the witnesses who could establish that Archie Stallings was a sexual predator, and Loretta Washington continued to refine the legal arguments Robin would make and drafted responses to the government's briefs in opposition to Jose's motion.

Robin kept Frank Melville up-to-date on the progress of the case and sent copies of any documents to Frank and Jose. Communicating with Frank Melville was easy, but Jose refused to meet with her.

Robin had hoped that Jose could set aside his anger, but there really wasn't anything he could contribute to the success of the case. Robin was alleging that Jose had nothing to do with Margo Prescott's murder and would win if she could convince the judge that Archie Stallings was the man who should have been sent to death row, and Jose's attorney had been incompetent when he failed to unearth and present numerous witnesses who would have been able to impeach Stallings's testimony, and might have laid a foundation for the prosecution of the key witness against Jose Alvarez.

Then, two weeks before the hearing, Jose had asked Robin to visit him. Robin had not asked why and hoped against hope that he wasn't going to ask her to cancel the hearing.

Once again, Robin was taken to the noncontact visiting room, where she waited nervously for her client to appear. When the door opened and the guard ushered Jose in, Robin searched his face for a clue to his feelings and saw none.

Robin decided to open the dialogue with a softball question.

"Have you read the pleadings, my memo, and the affidavits from Debra Porter and the other women?"

"Yes. You make a strong case."

"Let's hope the judge agrees. Your hearing is coming up in two weeks, and it's going to be in the federal courthouse in Portland. Unfortunately, you can't be transported because you're a security risk, so you'll be watching the proceedings on a television in the penitentiary. We'll be able to talk to each other on a secure line, and you'll be able to see and hear everything that goes on in court. Do you have any questions so far?"

"No, but I do have something I want to say. I was very angry the first time we met. I realize how badly I've treated you, and I want to apologize."

"No apology is necessary."

"But it is. You've done nothing but help me. You're the only one who has."

"Frank Melville is the person you should thank."

Jose's tone hardened. "I don't think I'll ever be able to do that. He kept his mouth shut when he should have told someone as soon as he learned I was innocent."

"He was bound by the attorney-client rule."

"That doesn't excuse what he did to me. He stole years of my life, when he knew I was innocent."

Robin realized that any discussion of the rules governing the attorney-client privilege would fall on deaf ears, so she changed the subject.

"The judge will be able to see you on TV, so I'm going to get you a suit so you'll look nice. You'll only be visible from the chest up, so no pants or shoes, and the authorities see ties as a no-no because they can be used as a weapon or for suicide. But you'll have a nice shirt and jacket."

Jose smiled. "I haven't worn anything decent in thirty years. It will seem strange."

"Let's hope that this won't be the last time you get to dress up."

The courtroom in the Mark O. Hatfield United States Courthouse where Jose's case was going to be heard had been completed in 1997. Despite the attempt to decorate it with soft, red woods and a tapestry depicting Oregon history, it tilted toward function over form. The state-of-the-art technology in the newer courtroom allowed Jose at OSP and Frank Melville at Black Oaks to participate remotely.

The Honorable Richard Davies, an African American, had been assigned the case. Davies was only forty-two, but he looked older. He wore wire-rimmed glasses, had a slight paunch and sloped shoulders, and walked with a cane. Davies had been a corporate lawyer with one of Portland's larger law firms. He was new to the bench, and no one had a good read on him yet.

Mary Kim, a veteran litigator in her early fifties, was the assistant attorney general who had been sent to represent the state of Oregon. Robin had gone up against her before and expected her to be thoroughly prepared.

"I've read your petition and accompanying memorandum of law and affidavits, Miss Lockwood," Judge Davies said. "This case appears to have many complex legal issues."

"I don't think it's that complicated, Your Honor," Robin replied. "At the heart of the case is the fact that Jose Alvarez has been rotting on death row for thirty years for a crime he did not commit. We're asking you to hear evidence that will convince you to let him go home."

Davies smiled. "That was nicely stated, but it avoids the problem of navigating a winding procedural road to arrive at that destination. For example, you concede that you can't bring your claim in state court because the statute of limitations has run. Why do you think this court has jurisdiction to hear the case?"

"Mr. Alvarez was accused of killing Margo Prescott. The key witness for the prosecution in Mr. Alvarez's trial was Archie Stallings. A few years after Mr. Alvarez was sentenced to death, Mr. Stallings was arrested and charged with rape. The detectives who investigated Stallings had no trouble finding several women who claimed he was a sexual predator.

"One woman, Debra Porter, was a close friend of Margo Prescott. She told the police that Stallings had pestered Prescott for sex and had tried to force her into a bedroom at a party. The person who saved her was Jose Alvarez.

"If Debra Porter had testified at Mr. Alvarez's trial, she would have damaged Mr. Stallings's credibility and would have had a major impact on the verdict. More important, she was easy to find. The fact that Mr. Alvarez's trial counsel did not find her and another woman who claimed that Stallings had molested her is a strong argument that Mr. Alvarez was denied competent counsel in violation of the Sixth Amendment right to counsel.

"These facts and our contention that Mr. Alvarez is completely innocent give this court the right to hear the case."

"Mrs. Kim?" the judge said.

"Mr. Stallings wasn't investigated until several years after Mr. Alvarez was convicted, so we don't know what the women would have said if they'd been interviewed when Mr. Alvarez was tried. I don't think you can fault Mr. Alvarez's trial attorney for not discovering them."

"What about Debra Porter?" Judge Davies asked. "She was a friend of the victim. You'd think Mr. Alvarez's lawyer would have known about her. If she'd been interviewed, can't we assume she would have given testimony that could have been used to impeach Mr. Stallings?"

"Well, yes, if you assume that she would have told the defense attorney what she told the detectives. She might not have wanted to help the person who the police were convinced murdered her friend.

"Which brings me to the biggest problem with Mr. Alvarez's case," Kim said. "There is no new evidence before this court that would clear Mr. Alvarez. All we have is an affidavit from Mr. Melville stating that he is in possession of some kind of evidence that would bear on the case, but can't tell anyone about it because it was an attorney-client confidence. My research has led me to conclude that the privilege exists after death. So, Miss Lockwood hasn't presented any evidence that Mr. Alvarez is really innocent."

"That is troubling, Miss Lockwood. Mrs. Kim's argument has a lot of merit."

"It's our position that Mr. Melville can reveal the contents of the confidential communication he had from his client," Robin said.

"Enlighten me, Miss Lockwood."

"There's an exception to the attorney-client privilege that would permit Mr. Melville to testify, and we believe it applies here. If a confidence involves a threat of future harm to an individual, an attorney is permitted to reveal it. For example, if Mrs. Kim hired me and told me in confidence that she was going to shoot you after this hearing, I would be permitted to reveal the confidence to prevent future harm coming to you."

"That exception doesn't apply here," Kim interjected. "The threat has to be an imminent one."

"I can't think of anyone who is in more imminent danger than Mr. Alvarez," Robin countered. "He's on death row and could be executed at any time."

"That's not true," Kim said. "Only two people have been executed in Oregon since the death penalty was reinstated in 1984. That was in 1996 and 1997. I don't think Mr. Alvarez is in any danger."

"Neither were federal prisoners until Donald Trump was elected president. There was wholesale slaughter at the end of his term. We have an election coming up. Who knows what the next governor will do?"

"None of us," Judge Davies said, "and I'm not going to base my decision on a forecast of the result of the next election. This case presents several complicated and serious issues, and I've concluded that I need to hear what Mr. Melville has to say in order to resolve them. So, I'm going to hear his testimony in my chambers without counsel present."

"I object, Your Honor," Kim said.

Davies smiled. "I assumed you would, but something Miss Lockwood said has touched me. We lawyers get so wrapped up in technicalities that we sometimes forget the real-world consequences of what we do. So, I ask you, Mrs. Kim, if Jose Alvarez is really, truly innocent, don't you want to set him free?"

Kim had been standing like a fighter; tense and tight in combat mode. The judge's words acted like a punch in the gut.

"I know I won't be able to live with myself," Judge Davies continued, "if I know I could have helped an innocent man who spent thirty years on death row for a crime he didn't commit and I didn't do something about it."

Twenty minutes later, Judge Davies returned to the bench. He looked grim.

"I'm going to permit Frank Melville to reveal the confidential communication he received from Archie Stallings," the judge said as the bailiff set up the television screen in the court so everyone could see Melville and hear him.

"I've concluded that Mr. Alvarez is in imminent danger as a result of being condemned to death, so I believe the exception to the privilege applies here."

"Objection on the grounds previously stated," Kim said.

"You've made your record, if the State decides to appeal."

Frank Melville appeared on the screen.

"Mr. Melville, please relate your contacts with Archie Stallings."

"Thank you for letting me do that, Your Honor. You have no idea how heavily it has weighed on me to have had to keep what I know to myself.

"When I was a prosecutor in the Multnomah County district attorney's office, I prosecuted Jose Alvarez for the murder of Margo Prescott. I met Archie Stallings for the first time when he was a witness against Mr. Alvarez. He testified that he saw Mr. Alvarez running from the scene of the crime with blood on his person around the time that the medical examiner established that Margo Prescott had been killed.

"My next contact with Mr. Stallings came when I left the district attorney's office to go into private practice. He hired me to represent him when he was charged with rape. After I won his case, we returned to my office, and he told me that he met Margo Prescott outside her dormitory on the evening of her murder. She was upset because she and Mr. Alvarez had quarreled.

"Mr. Stallings confessed that he had been trying to have sex with Miss Prescott for some time, and she had always rejected his advances. He saw her as emotionally vulnerable because of the breakup with Mr. Alvarez and pretended to be sympathetic. Once they were in Miss Prescott's dorm room, Mr. Stallings told me that he attempted to have sex with her. When she resisted, he hit her. He told me that he panicked because he was afraid that she would report him to the police, so he killed her.

"As he was leaving the crime scene, Mr. Stallings saw Mr. Alvarez coming up the stairs. He hid before slipping out of the dormitory when Mr. Alvarez went into Miss Prescott's room."

"What did you do after hearing Mr. Stallings's confession?" Judge Davies asked.

"I told him that he had to go to the authorities and clear Mr. Alvarez's name. He refused. He said he'd done some research and knew that I couldn't reveal his confidential communication. He also said that he would deny telling me that he had murdered Miss Prescott if I told anyone, and he'd see I was disbarred.

"Over the years, I tried to convince Mr. Stallings to do the right thing, but, in my opinion, he was a sociopath who relished the fact that he had put me in a bind."

"Do you have any questions for Mr. Melville, Mrs. Kim?"

"How do you know that Mr. Stallings was telling you the truth? You said that he was a sociopath. What if he was having fun at your expense and really had not killed Miss Prescott?"

Melville paused to consider the question. "There are a few things that make me believe he was telling the truth. First, Mr. Alvarez always said he was innocent. I offered him a plea that would have let him escape the death penalty, and he rejected it. When he testified at his trial, he was very convincing."

"Obviously not convincing enough," Kim said, "since the jury not only found him guilty, but sentenced him to die."

The color drained from Melville's face. "That's on me, Mrs. Kim. I was an exceptional attorney and a master orator. The closing argument in Mr. Alvarez's case was one of the best I have ever given."

"Or maybe Mr. Alvarez was not so convincing."

"How do you explain the hammer?" Melville asked.

Kim looked confused. "What hammer?"

"Miss Prescott was killed with blows from a hammer. The police never found the weapon. Stallings said that he took it with him and threw it in the Willamette River. The police learned that Miss Prescott borrowed a hammer to hang a picture, but that didn't come out at trial for some reason. The medical examiner never specified the weapon that had been used. Stallings told me that there was a framed picture of Mount Hood on Miss Prescott's bed along with a nail and a hammer. How would he know that if he wasn't in her room?"

Kim started to say something. Then she stopped.

"Nothing further, Your Honor."

"Miss Lockwood?"

"No questions."

"Thank you, Mr. Melville," Judge Davies said.

The judge turned to the attorneys. "You can make closing arguments if you want to, but I think I have all of the information I need to rule in this case."

"I'm good, Your Honor, unless you have questions for me," Robin said.

"Mrs. Kim?"

The assistant AG looked troubled. "I don't have anything to add."

"Then court is in recess."

A text from Jose appeared on Robin's phone. *What is he going to do?*

Robin spoke into the phone she was using to connect with her client.

"I gave up predicting the outcome of court cases a long time ago, but Mr. Melville was great, and that business with the hammer was very powerful. Hopefully, the judge will rule soon, and, fingers crossed, you'll be a free man."

CHAPTER TWELVE

A month after the hearing in Jose's case, Robin's receptionist told her that Judge Davies's secretary was on the line.

"Hi," Robin said, trying not to sound anxious while her heart pounded like a trip hammer.

"The judge would like you in court at nine tomorrow. Is that convenient?"

When a federal judge asked if you could make time for him, he was just being polite. Federal judges had God status, and litigants had to be where they were told even if they were scheduled to give birth or have a lifesaving operation.

"I'll be there. Are you going to arrange for Mr. Alvarez and Mr. Melville to be hooked up remotely?"

"We're on it," the secretary said.

Robin called Black Oaks as soon as she hung up. Frank Melville answered the phone.

"Something important has happened in the Alvarez case," Robin said.

"Did we win?"

"I don't know. But the judge wants everyone in court tomorrow. His office will probably be in touch soon to set up the link to his courtroom."

"Thank you, Robin, for everything you've done."

"I haven't done anything yet."

"I'm not talking about winning. I don't know if there are many lawyers who could have gotten this far."

"I didn't do it on my own, and we'll be back to square one or worse, if the judge rules against Jose."

Robin's gut was in a knot when Judge Davies's bailiff called the court to order. Robin could hear Jose's labored breathing on the cell phone that lay within reach on her counsel table, and she could see the tension on Frank Melville's face on the monitor that was broadcasting from Black Oaks.

Judge Davies did not look at Robin or Mary Kim when he limped onto the dais. He took his seat, leaned his cane against his chair, and looked down at a sheaf of papers he held in his hand. After studying them for a few minutes, the judge looked across the courtroom.

"As you know, I'm new to the bench. When I received this appointment, I was eager to start hearing cases, deciding interesting issues of constitutional law, and trying to do justice for those who came into my court. I was very excited, but I was also very naïve, and every decision I've made so far has been very easy. It never occurred to me that at some point in my career on the bench I would be required to make a decision of the magnitude of the one I will be making in this case.

"When I read the pleadings and legal memos Miss Lockwood and Mrs. Kim submitted, I saw the case the way most judges do as a battle of competing legal issues. Did this court have jurisdiction? Would Mr. Melville be allowed to tell me something a client had told him in confidence? Then we held the hearing and I listened to Mr. Melville, and I realized that I had to stop thinking like a lawyer and start thinking about the impact that a liar's testimony had on the life of a young, talented human being.

"Jose Alvarez came up through poverty. His parents sacrificed everything so he could have the life they never had, and Archie Stallings destroyed their dreams.

"I am going to grant Mr. Alvarez's motion. I hope the case ends with his freedom. Even more, I hope that he can salvage his future.

"Mrs. Kim, the legal issues you have raised are valid, but I hope, when you discuss how you should proceed in this case with the attorney general, that you try to view this case not as an attorney, but as a human being who can do something good for a person who has been horribly wronged."

Frank Melville's face was visible on a monitor, and Robin could see tears streaming down his cheeks. Jose was visible on another monitor. He looked shell-shocked. Robin picked up the phone that connected her to Jose.

"Did you understand what just happened?" she asked.

"They're going to let me out?" Jose asked, as if he was not completely convinced.

"Not right away. There were a lot of complex legal issues that were raised in your case, and the State has the right to appeal the judge's decision. An appellate court could decide that the judge was wrong on the law and reverse him. Both sides could eventually end up in the United States Supreme Court. In the worst-case scenario, you could still be living on death row. And, even if we win eventually, the case could drag on for years. But Judge Davies made a powerful argument on your behalf. He'll have fleshed it out and expanded it in his written decision. I'm hoping that the AG's office decides to do justice and decides not to appeal."

"When will we know?" Jose asked.

"Don't sit by the phone, Jose. Making a decision on an appeal could take months. Just keep your fingers crossed and your hopes in check."

CHAPTER THIRTEEN

"You did it!" Robin told Frank Melville. "Mary Kim just called me. The attorney general decided that there was a good possibility that Jose was innocent, and the State isn't going to appeal. Jose is going to be free."

There was silence on the line. Then Robin heard an intake of breath followed by the sound of her client crying.

"I don't know how to thank you," Melville said when he had regained his composure.

"You don't have to. Freeing an innocent person from death row is the best present a defense attorney can get."

"What will Jose do now?" Melville asked.

"I don't know. I'm headed down to Salem as soon as we hang up to tell him the news, and I'll ask. Both of his parents passed. I don't know about any other relatives, and I doubt he has any friends he can rely on after thirty years in prison."

"He has one person he can rely on. Tell Jose I'll take care of him. I'll pay for a room at the best hotel in Portland until he can find a place to live, I'll cover his food and pay for new clothes, and I'll use my contacts to get him a good job."

"That's very generous of you."

"It's poor compensation for what Jose has suffered."

"I'm sure he'll be grateful," Robin said, although she wasn't sure how Jose would react, knowing the anger he displayed whenever she mentioned Frank Melville's name.

"I want to meet Jose," Melville said. "I want you to bring him to Black Oaks to celebrate his freedom. You must come too. And bring Mr. Breland. I was very impressed by his investigative skills, and I may have more work for you two."

Two hours after Robin ended her call to Frank Melville, she was seated on the attorney side of the non-contact visiting room at the Oregon State Penitentiary.

"It's over," Robin said when Jose picked up the receiver.

Jose stared through the bulletproof glass as if he had not heard what Robin had just said.

"We won," Robin explained. "The State isn't going to appeal Judge Davies's decision. You're going to be free."

Jose continued to stare. Robin smiled.

"This is not a dream, Jose. It's real. You'll be released tomorrow, and I'll be here to pick you up."

Jose sucked in a breath. Then tears began streaming down his cheeks. He drew his arm across his face to wipe them away.

"I told Mr. Melville about the State's decision before I drove down. He's putting you up at a very nice hotel in Portland and paying all of your expenses while we try to find you a place to live. He wants me to drive you to Black Oaks to discuss your future. Mr. Melville wants to know if you want to finish your college degree or find a job. Think that over. We won't be going before the weekend."

Jose's features hardened. "I don't know if I want his help."

Robin stopped smiling and leaned forward. "We've talked about this, Jose. You have to let go of your anger toward Mr. Melville. You know that there was nothing he could have done until Stallings died. And once he knew Stallings was dead, he did everything he could to set you free.

"Holding a grudge will only hurt you. Your pride has kept you going all these years, but you can't let it stand in the way of accepting the help you need to get back on your feet."

Jose looked down. "I have to think."

"You have to be realistic. You need a place to stay. You need clothes. No one else is going to feed and house you once you leave this prison. Frank Melville is trying to make up for the wrong that was done to you in every way he can. Forgive him. Let him help you."

Robin stopped talking. It dawned on her that Jose had to be overwhelmed by the news that he would soon be off death row, out of OSP and free for the first time in thirty years.

"I'm sorry," she apologized. "I shouldn't have lectured you. I'll be waiting when you're released. Is there someone you want me to call?"

Jose shook his head. "My folks passed away. I had a brother and sister. They visited when I was on trial. My sister visited for a while after I was convicted, but everyone stopped writing or coming after a few years. My brother passed away, but I don't know where my sister lives or if she's still alive."

"Okay. We can try and track her down. And I'll help any way I can."

"I know you will. I also know that I owe my life to you."

Robin was tempted to say that he owed his life to Frank Melville, but she was savvy enough to keep that thought to herself.

CHAPTER FOURTEEN

The state of Oregon west of the Cascade Range has two seasons. In the middle of the year, the state is a verdant, sunny, multicolored botanical garden where every variety of flower, tree, and bush is displayed against a backdrop of snowcapped mountains and winding rivers. But you can't have the green without a lot of water, and the rest of the year the mountains disappear behind dark, threatening clouds, and the heavens open to discharge a constant, depressing rain.

It saddened Robin that after thirty years of being locked in a narrow, dark cell, Jose was not going to walk out of the penitentiary when the sky was blue, the sun was shining, and the world was a riot of color, but Jose handled the inclement weather well. When he stepped out of the prison into a soggy, cold drizzle, he turned his face into the rain, breathed in the air of freedom, and smiled.

They headed down the path to the parking lot, and Robin noticed the spring in Jose's step.

"You look like you're in pretty good shape for someone who's been fed a diet of prison food for thirty years," she said, smiling. "How did you manage?"

Jose smiled. "Lots of push-ups and lots of sit-ups. It helped pass the time."

Jose was dressed in a fresh set of clothes that Robin had brought to the prison. She used an umbrella to protect them as she led Jose to her car. Robin ducked into the driver's seat to get out of the rain. Jose paused outside the passenger door and looked at sights that had been hidden from him from the moment he was herded into the prison.

"Mr. Melville has you in a suite at the Jefferson Hotel, one of Portland's finest," Robin said when she drove out of the visitors' lot and headed toward I-5 north.

"That's very kind of him," Jose said, but there was no trace of gratitude in the flat reply.

"I'll be at the Jefferson on Saturday for the trip to Black Oaks. That'll give you a few days to adjust to life as a free man."

Jose didn't say anything. Robin didn't push him, and they traveled the rest of the way to the hotel with very little conversation.

When Robin exited the highway, Jose stared at the crowds on the streets and the skyscrapers that had not existed the last time he was in Portland. A few minutes later, Robin parked in front of the Jefferson Hotel, a modern glass-and-steel affair. Jose looked very uncomfortable when they walked into the spacious atrium in the hotel lobby. He had grown up in poverty in a tiny apartment in a housing project. Being in this grand space with so much light and fresh air would probably have been unsettling even if he had never been incarcerated.

Robin empathized with him. She'd grown up in Elk Grove, a small farming town in the Midwest, and had been overwhelmed and disoriented by the crowds, glitter, and noise in the lobby of the Las Vegas casino where she had her first televised pay-per-view fight.

Robin helped Jose check in before escorting him to his suite. She showed him how to use the key card, then stepped aside to let him in. Jose hesitated before walking into the sitting room with its massive television. The drapes on the floor-to-ceiling windows were open. Jose walked up to the window and stared out. Robin hung back and watched him. Jose placed a hand on the glass. Then, without a word, he turned away and walked into a bedroom with its king-sized bed and second television.

"I'm guessing this is a little different from your cell," Robin said, trying to lighten the situation.

Jose didn't smile. He walked into the bathroom and stared at the glass-enclosed shower and massive tub. Then he walked back into the bedroom and dropped onto the bed. He looked scared.

Robin sat next to him. "Don't let this overwhelm you. You were an engineering student. This is just stuff. You'll figure out how it works pretty quickly. I'll show you the lights, the temperature controls, and how to work the remote. The TV has a lot of new gadgets, like streaming and cable channels, but it's still a TV."

Jose continued to look at the floor. His breathing was shallow.

"Are you hungry?" Robin asked.

He didn't answer.

"Let's get you some lunch," Robin said. "You're going to enjoy having choices, and you're really going to enjoy food that doesn't taste like the shit you've been eating. What do you say?"

"This is too much," he whispered.

"No, Jose. This is what would have been normal for you if Archie Stallings didn't lie at your trial. You would have been a successful engineer who would have stayed in places just like this when you went on vacation. Life dealt you a very bad hand, but you have it in your power to start over, if you can look forward instead of looking back."

PART FIVE

THE BLACK OAKS CURSE

CHAPTER FIFTEEN

The windshield wipers in the rental car were losing their battle with a torrential rain that was making it almost impossible to see the narrow, treacherous road. Another hairpin turn appeared out of nowhere, and Corey Rockwell's gut clenched again. He slowed down, made the turn, and caught his breath, thankful that he hadn't plunged over the edge of the cliff that was oh so close.

This was complete bullshit, Rockwell thought. He could not believe that he'd had to rent a car. In his heyday, a chauffeured limousine would have been waiting for him at the airport. Maybe his films weren't grossing what they used to, but he was still a star. At least two people had stared at him when he got off the plane, and he was certain that more had whispered about him when he was waiting at baggage claim.

That was another thing that had put him in a foul mood. He wasn't used to flying commercial, and certainly not in economy. And he was used to having an assistant collect his luggage. But he couldn't afford an assistant just now, although he was certain that was a temporary inconvenience.

Frank Melville had paid for Rockwell's airfare and the rental car, but Rockwell was still pissed off because Melville hadn't come to Hollywood to negotiate the terms of the film deal. Melville's assistant had told him that Melville was partially paralyzed, but lots of cripples flew on planes. Melville wanted to do a film about Corey's life, so he should have come to Corey, instead of making him navigate the most terrifying terrain he'd ever driven outside of one of his movies. Although, to be honest, he hadn't really driven the cars in the chase scenes. When there was a car chase on roads like this in one of his movies, a stuntman had risked his life while Corey stayed in his trailer screwing some starlet.

Rockwell had been reluctant to do the film at first. Let sleeping dogs lie, he'd thought. Why dig up all the rumors about his wife's murder? But he hadn't made a film in a while, and his savings were dwindling. Necessity was the mother of something or other. Once Frank Melville financed his film and paid him what he deserved for starring in it, the universe would right itself, and he'd be back on top, riding in limousines once again, instead of this shitty Ford. And he really had nothing to worry about. The jury had convicted that guy. What was his name? Who cared? There was no new evidence, so no one was going to reopen the case. That asshole was on death row, and Corey Rockwell was free as a bird.

Melville had assured him that the film was going to focus on his grief and loss, so he'd be a sympathetic character, not a suspect. And the film would be serious, not like his action thrillers. Maybe the movie would breathe new life into his career and showcase his talents as a dramatic actor.

Rockwell made one last turn, saw a stone wall and a metal gate, and thanked God that he'd made it up the mountain in one piece. Rockwell pressed the button on the intercom. Moments later, a gravelly voice asked for his name. He gave it, the gate opened, and Rockwell drove along a winding driveway to a house that looked like every spooky mansion in every horror movie.

Rockwell parked, grabbed his overnight bag, hunched his shoulders, and raced through the rain to the shelter provided by the portico. Just as he was about to use the metal knocker, the front door opened, and he found himself staring at Beauty and the Beast.

"Come in, Mr. Rockwell," said a honey-haired blonde who was the equal of any of the actresses who had played opposite him in one of his action thrillers. Behind her lurked a scarred giant who could have played the villain's henchman in those same films.

"I'm Sheila Monroe, Mr. Melville's assistant. We talked on the phone."

"Of course," Rockwell said as he mentally undressed Monroe.

"I apologize for the weather and the awful road you had to navigate."

Rockwell flashed his famous smile. "I can hardly hold you responsible for the elements. They're God's doing. I'm sure there would have been blue skies and smooth going if you were in charge."

Sheila laughed. Then she turned to the giant.

"This is Luther, our houseman. He'll show you to your room. Are you hungry?"

"Famished. Any chance I can get a very stiff drink? A really good single-malt scotch if you've got one. After the ride up the mountain, I need something to steady my nerves."

"That shouldn't be a problem. I'll have Luther bring you something I think you'll enjoy."

"I will be eternally grateful," Rockwell said as he looked into Monroe's blue eyes. Monroe responded with a warm smile, and Rockwell was certain that she was sending signals. A woman like Monroe living in a creepy place like this with a guy in a wheelchair and a movie monster was probably aching to hop into the sack with a real man.

"Mr. Melville is anxious to meet you," Sheila said. "I'll have lunch brought up while you change out of your travel clothes. Then I'll take you to meet him."

Sheila turned and walked down the gloomy corridor that led away from the entry hall. Rockwell handed Luther his bag and admired Monroe's backside as he followed the houseman. Maybe this wouldn't be such a bad couple of days, after all, he thought.

* * *

A tray with a hot meal and a glass of excellent scotch was waiting for Rockwell by the time he finished showering and changing into a black turtleneck, black slacks, and a black leather jacket, which were the clothes Rocky Slate, the hero of the Hard to Kill movies, always wore. He was just finishing his meal when Sheila Monroe knocked on his door.

"Come in," Rockwell said.

"Are you ready to meet your host?" Sheila asked.

"Take me to him."

Sheila turned, and the actor followed her down the hall to the far end of the other third-floor wing. Sheila opened a door and stepped back to let Rockwell into Frank Melville's office. Melville was seated in his wheelchair behind his desk. He was wearing a navy-blue pinstriped jacket over a white shirt and blue-and-red-striped tie.

"Please come in, Mr. Rockwell. And thank you for coming to Black Oaks. I appreciate the sacrifice, and I hope I can reward you for it by financing a movie that will rekindle your career."

Rockwell didn't like the fact that Melville thought his career needed rekindling, but he wasn't going to correct the man who might be financing his next film. Rockwell took a seat across from his host, and Sheila sat next to him.

"Has Miss Monroe seen to your needs?" Melville asked.

"She's been great."

"And your room? Is it okay?"

"It's very nice. So," Rockwell said, anxious to finish the small talk and get down to business, "I have to say that I'm very excited by your movie idea, Mr. Melville. What inspired it?"

"I started my career as a prosecutor, and I specialized in prosecuting death penalty cases. After my accident, I came to realize that there were innocent people who had been sentenced to death, and I've dedicated myself to finding these men and women and helping gain their freedom."

"That's very noble of you."

"While Miss Monroe and I were investigating these cases, we learned about the murder of your wife, Claire Winters."

Rockwell frowned. "There's no mystery about who killed my dear wife."

"I agree wholeheartedly. The man who was convicted for that heinous crime is where he belongs."

Rockwell relaxed.

"But your tragedy touched me. Here was a man who had fame and fortune, but what was that worth when he obtained it at the cost of losing the woman he loved?"

"You got that right. I'd give everything back—the career, the money, the fame—if I could have my Claire back in my arms."

"Yes, exactly," Melville said. "And, because of that, I saw all the elements of a great film. We have the murder of a beautiful movie star, the successful investigation and conviction of the man who committed it, and the impact of that horrible crime on you.

"Of course, you will be the focus of the film. The murder, the investigation, and the trial would be a subplot. The conflict between the fame the murder brought you and your anguish at the loss of your wife would be what we would concentrate on. So, now that you've heard my idea, what do you think?"

"I think it's great, and I can't wait to jump in."

Melville beamed. "I'd hoped you'd feel that way. Now, I've been doing some research into the motion picture industry, and I'm guessing that the first thing we need to do is find someone to write the screenplay."

"And financing. A good script is important, but finding the money is what makes a project go from an idea to the silver screen."

Melville nodded. "I'm way ahead of you. I had a successful career in private practice after I left the district attorney's office, and my investments have done very well, so I can help fund our project. I've also talked with some people with deep pockets who are definitely interested in contributing capital."

"That's great!"

"Do you have an idea for a screenwriter?"

"Let me give it some thought."

"Excellent. Now I believe that we should give the writer as much background material as we can, and I've compiled a list of people who were involved in the case who we want to interview. These would be the detectives, the witnesses, etcetera."

Melville swiveled his chair and took a thick file out of a cabinet behind his desk. He studied it for a moment.

"We do have names and addresses for some of them, but we're having trouble locating some of the people who would be characters in the movie."

"I haven't kept in touch with the cops or the prosecutors," Rockwell said. "The DA's office and the precinct can probably put you in touch."

"That's a great idea. There are two people we can't trace. They're the people who were with you on the evening of the murder."

Melville looked down at his file. "One is your old stuntman, Tony Clark, and the other is his neighbor, Rose McIntire. Do you know where we can find either of them?"

Rockwell's pulse quickened, but he kept his composure.

"I'm afraid I can't help you there. I only met Miss McIntire once. She was Tony's neighbor and a fan, so he invited her over. I got her a few parts in some of my films, but I haven't seen her in ages."

"And Mr. Clark?"

"Yeah. Tony quit the stuntman business after we filmed *Hard to Kill,* and I lost contact." Rockwell shrugged. "We worked together and I liked the guy, but we were never close."

Melville looked surprised. "I heard that Mr. Clark wanted to open a bar, and you helped him out with some money."

"That's true. I was flush with cash after *Hard to*

Kill became a megahit, and a lot of people came to me with their hand out. Tony was a good guy so I loaned him some cash. I can't even remember how much."

"Oh, it was a loan?"

"Yeah, but he never paid me back. Like I said, we didn't keep in touch after he quit the movie business."

"Okay. If you do remember anything or think of other people we should talk to—people who could tell us how Claire's death affected you—please tell Miss Monroe or me."

"Will do."

"And now, I am guessing, you'd like to discuss your compensation."

CHAPTER SIXTEEN

Frank Melville had insisted on celebrating Jose's freedom at Black Oaks, and it had taken all of Robin's powers of persuasion to convince Jose to go. On Saturday morning, Robin parked in front of the Jefferson just as a light rain started to fall. Jose got into the passenger seat. Ken Breland was sitting in back.

"Are you surviving normal life?" Ken asked as Robin pulled into traffic.

"Yeah, but it's not easy."

"What's the biggest difficulty?" Ken asked.

"All the choices. Every day was the same on death row, and someone always told me what I could and couldn't do. Now I have to decide when I go to bed, when I get up, what I want to do during the day. And everything works on a computer. I get so frustrated."

Ken smiled. "Computers frustrate everyone our age. But you're a smart guy. You'll figure it out."

Jose laughed. "I don't know. I still haven't figured out the TV."

"Join the club," Ken said. "And always remember that Robin and I are here to help you with the TV or anything else."

Robin had been relieved to hear Jose make a joke, but that was the last light moment on the trip to Black Oaks. Jose spent the rest of the ride staring out of his window at scenery that had been hidden from his view for so long. Then they passed the hospital for the criminally insane, and his features darkened.

Moments after they passed the asylum, they started the climb to the summit of Solitude Mountain, and the light rain that had greeted Jose outside the Jefferson transformed into a torrential downpour. Jose looked over the side of the cliff and pressed against the car door. Robin didn't blame him. The rain was loosening the soil on the cliffside, and small rocks fell on the roadway and ricocheted off the car.

Robin used the call box to announce their arrival. Moments later, the metal gate swung open to admit them. Robin had tried to prepare Jose for Black Oaks during the ride by giving him a description of the manor house and telling him the legend, but Jose still stared when they rounded a turn and a bolt of lightning lit up the mansion.

"What is this place?" Jose asked.

"Weird, huh?" Ken said.

"It's even creepier inside," Robin said. "And don't gawk at Luther, if he lets us in. He's the houseman.

He's huge, and one side of his face is horribly scarred, I'm guessing by a fire."

The front door opened when Robin parked her car, and she could see Luther and Mrs. Raskin standing in the hall. Ken ran inside, but Jose stayed in the car. Robin pulled up the hood on her jacket to ward off the rain and opened his door.

"Come on. Let's get out of this downpour," she said.

Jose hesitated. Then he climbed out and followed Robin into Black Oaks. As soon as they were in the entryway, Luther stepped aside to reveal Nelly Melville standing behind her father. Frank rolled his wheelchair forward.

"I'm so happy that you can enter Black Oaks as a free man, Mr. Alvarez."

Jose mumbled a thank-you, clearly embarrassed by the attention and torn by his feelings for the man who was responsible for his freedom.

"This is my daughter, Nelly."

"Welcome to Black Oaks," Nelly said, gracing Jose with a warm, welcoming smile. Except for his lawyer, Jose hadn't been the recipient of a beautiful woman's smile in thirty years, and he felt heat in his cheeks.

"Mrs. Raskin will show you to your rooms," Frank Melville said. "When you've freshened up, I'd like the three of you to meet me in my office."

Melville rolled out of the way, and the trio followed Mrs. Raskin. Robin paused when she came to the hanging that showed the wolf hunt. There was something else that Robin had missed the first time she'd seen the tapestry. The lead hunter was mounted on a coal-black steed and carrying a knife with a silver blade and a handle that looked half-wolf's claw, half-human.

"Remember what I told you about the legend of Black Oaks?"

"The werewolves and the devil worship?"

"Exactly. Look at this tapestry. It's a copy of a tapestry that hangs in the original manor house in Sexton, England." Robin pointed at the wolf. "It's half-human and half-wolf. And look at the knife the hunter is holding."

Jose looked where Robin was pointing. Then he smiled and shook his head.

"This place is really creepy."

"My feelings exactly. Only don't mention the legend or the Black Oaks curse to Mr. Melville. His daughter told me that he takes the curse very seriously."

Mrs. Raskin had stopped in the hallway when Robin was showing the tapestry to Jose. When Robin turned away from the tapestry, Mrs. Raskin continued down the corridor. Robin, Ken, and Jose caught up with Mrs. Raskin when she stopped in front of the staircase and the elevator. Mrs. Raskin went into the elevator, and Ken followed her. Jose started to follow Ken, but Robin stopped him.

"There's not enough room in the elevator for the four of us and our bags," Robin said as she tossed her bag into the cage. "Ken, why don't you ride up with Mrs. Raskin and the bags? Jose and I will take the stairs."

Jose handed his bag to Ken. Mrs. Raskin pressed the button for the third floor. When she shut the gate, the elevator rose slowly, and Jose was level with it when it jerked to a stop between the second and third floors before continuing on its way. Robin turned to Jose.

"The last time I was here Mrs. Raskin said that happens frequently, and she predicted a fatal crash, which is why I chose to use the stairs. You can thank me for saving your life again."

Jose smiled. It was the second time Robin had seen any sign of happiness. She hoped that it wouldn't be the last.

Robin and Jose waited for the elevator on the third-floor landing. Mrs. Raskin got out and opened a door across from the elevator.

"You'll be staying in this room, Mr. Alvarez. Why don't you go in and I'll tell you everything you need to know after I get Miss Lockwood and Mr. Breland settled."

Jose entered the room, and Mrs. Raskin turned to Robin.

"I put you in the room you occupied during your first visit," Mrs. Raskin told Robin. "Mr. Breland, you'll have the room next to Miss Lockwood."

Robin went inside her room and set her bag down on the bed. A thunderclap brought her to the window. The storm had created havoc during the ride to the manor house, and it looked like it was gaining in intensity. The tops of the trees at the edge of the lawn were swaying back and forth, and the wind was blow-ing with so much force that the rain was moving sideways. The howling sound it made still reminded her of a wolf baying. Robin scolded herself for having an overactive imagination and pulled herself away from the window.

CHAPTER SEVENTEEN

Most people would have wondered why a person as beautiful and accomplished as Sheila Monroe would isolate herself at the top of a mountain in the middle of nowhere. But Sheila had her reasons. After dinner last night, Frank Melville had visited her in her room. By the time he left, Sheila knew that everything she had worked for was about to come true.

Sheila had grown up dirt-poor with two assets, her brains and her looks, and she had decided at an early age that she was going to use them to get what she wanted by any means necessary. Manipulating Frank Melville to fall in love with her had taken time, but anyone living in this mausoleum had plenty of time on their hands.

Sheila had a friend who worked in an upscale employment agency. Her friend had told her about the research assistant job at Black Oaks as soon as Nelly Melville contacted the agency. Sheila had excellent research skills, and she'd decided that a wealthy man who had lost his wife and was confined to a wheelchair would be an easy mark; even one as obviously intelligent as Frank Melville. From experience, Sheila knew that a high IQ was no match for someone with her looks.

There was one more thing Sheila needed to have happen to make her plan work. When Justin Trent arrived at Black Oaks yesterday, Sheila was certain that everything was on track.

Frank had wanted her to join him when he went downstairs to welcome Jose Alvarez to Black Oaks, but Sheila had begged off with the excuse that she wanted to change before he met with Alvarez, Lockwood, and Breland. What Sheila did not tell Frank was that there was another reason she wanted to stay on the Melvilles' wing.

Sheila knew that Justin Trent, the son of Lawrence Trent, Frank's old law partner, was in love with Nelly Melville, so the young attorney's trip from Portland to the manor house was probably motivated in part by a desire to see her. But Sheila suspected that there may have been another reason Trent had traveled to Black Oaks. Justin specialized in probate law, and attorneys who practiced probate wrote wills. Frank had spent an hour alone with Trent before dinner.

Trent's room was next to Sheila's in the Melville wing. Before dinner, but after Trent's meeting with Frank, Nelly had gone to Trent's room. Sheila had overheard Trent and Nelly arguing, though she could not make out what they were saying. Sheila hoped that

Nelly was worried about something Frank had told Trent during their meeting. She also wanted to know if anything they had discussed concerned her.

As soon as Nelly and Frank went downstairs to greet Jose Alvarez, Sheila went into the hall and knocked on Trent's door. He was infatuated with Nelly and had always been impervious to Sheila's charms, so Sheila knew she was going to have to work hard to find out what had happened when Trent and Frank had met.

"One second!" Trent yelled.

Sheila stepped back, and the door opened. Trent was wearing slacks and a white shirt.

"Hi, Justin, getting ready to meet the guest of honor?"

"The guy Frank sprung from death row?" Trent said.

Sheila nodded.

"I don't know much about his situation. I read a piece in the newspaper, but that's about it."

"Oh, I'm surprised. Didn't Frank fill you in when you two met last night?"

"Frank told me he was coming up from Portland with his lawyer."

"I thought you and Frank were meeting because Frank is going to set up a trust or make some provision in his will for Jose."

Justin frowned. "You know I can't tell you what we talked about."

"Of course. I just wondered because Frank feels so bad about what happened to Alvarez."

"If he wants you to know what we discussed he'll tell you."

"Frank is meeting Jose in half an hour. Are you going to be there?"

"He hasn't asked me."

"Okay, then. I'll see you at dinner."

Trent closed the door, and Sheila looked at her watch. Frank had asked her to bring Alvarez, Lockwood, and Lockwood's investigator to his office. She looked down the hall and saw the trio with Mrs. Raskin. She decided to give them time to freshen up from their trip, before she got them.

CHAPTER EIGHTEEN

Robin had worn jeans, a long-sleeve shirt, and a sweater so she would be comfortable during the long trip to Black Oaks. After washing up, she changed into a black pants suit and white, man-tailored shirt and walked into the hall just as a door to one of the other rooms opened, and Corey Rockwell appeared on the landing.

Robin was surprised to see the actor at Black Oaks, and she was even more surprised to see how short he was. On screen, he seemed to be a towering presence. In real life, Robin had a few inches on him.

And there was another difference between the Corey Rockwell of the silver screen and the real-life Rockwell. In his movies, Rockwell always had a scene where he was bare-chested so he could show off his rippling muscles. If those scenes were included in his made-for-*Netflix* films, Robin guessed they featured a body double. The Rockwell who faced her showed the beginnings of a paunch, and the skin on his face, which used to look chiseled from granite, was loose. There were also signs of an overindulgence in alcohol.

Jeff had loved action movies, and Rockwell had a brief moment in the spotlight when he'd starred in *Hard to Kill,* the highest-grossing movie in the year it came out. It had been followed by *Hard to Kill II* and *Harder to Kill,* and Rockwell had been on his way to the summit of action-movie Olympus. Then drugs and a sex scandal involving a minor had derailed his career. Now his infrequent grade-C movies went straight to streaming channels.

Robin remembered Jeff telling her that a tragedy had been responsible for Rockwell's early success. He'd said that Rockwell had been married to a movie star who was murdered before the release of *Hard to Kill.* Robin couldn't remember her name, but Jeff had told her that her killer had been tried right around the time *Hard to Kill* had been released, and the publicity had made the movie an unexpected hit.

Rockwell sucked in his gut and flashed a smile at Robin.

"Hi there. Are you auditioning for the film?" he asked.

"What film?" Robin answered.

"The one Melville is financing for me. You're so attractive I assumed you were an actress."

"Thanks for the compliment, but I'm an attorney."

"Brains and beauty," Rockwell said, as he ran his eyes over Robin's body. "I'm Corey Rockwell."

"Robin Lockwood."

Rockwell's brow furrowed. "That sounds familiar."

"Have you ever been charged with a crime in Portland?" Robin asked with an impish smile.

Rockwell laughed. "Not that I remember, but there are several days that are a complete mystery to me."

Robin laughed just as the elevator arrived at their floor.

Rockwell held the sliding gate open for Robin.

"After you," he said.

"I'm not going downstairs. I'm meeting Mr. Melville."

At that moment, Sheila Monroe walked onto the landing from the wing with the Melville family rooms.

"I'd advise you to tread carefully where Miss Lockwood is involved," Sheila said. "She used to be a professional fighter."

Rockwell snapped his fingers. "Of course. You're Rockin' Robin Lockwood."

"Not for some time, Mr. Rockwell. Now I'm just plain old Robin Lockwood, Esquire."

Rockwell got into the elevator. As soon as it descended far enough so Robin didn't think Rockwell could hear her, she turned to Monroe.

"Please don't seat me next to Rockwell at dinner."

Monroe laughed. "I'll make sure there's a buffer zone between the two of you. He's already come on to me and Nelly, and he only just arrived."

"Rockwell said that Mr. Melville is financing a film project."

"There's more to it. That's one of the reasons Mr. Melville wanted you to bring Mr. Breland along."

"Oh?"

"Mr. Melville will fill you in when he's ready," Monroe said.

"Will there be any other surprise guests at the dinner?"

"No surprises, but Justin Trent is joining us. He's Mr. Melville's attorney and the son of the late Lawrence Trent, his former partner. And now let's collect your investigator and Mr. Alvarez. Mr. Melville is anxious to talk to you."

When Jose, Robin, and Ken Breland were seated across from him, Frank Melville addressed Jose, who looked very uncomfortable.

"When I asked Miss Lockwood to bring you here, she told me that she wasn't sure you would come. I know this was a difficult choice for you, and I want to thank you for deciding to meet me at Black Oaks."

Melville paused and waited for Jose to respond. When he didn't, Melville forged on.

"I don't blame you for being angry. I've been sick about your situation since Stallings confessed. Miss Lockwood has told you why my hands were tied. If I'd gone to the authorities and claimed that Stallings had confessed to killing Miss Prescott, he would have denied it. If I'd persisted, any court would have barred my testimony because an attorney cannot reveal what a client tells him in confidence. There was no way I could think of to tell anyone about Stallings's confession."

Jose stared at Melville for a moment. Then he

said, "Miss Lockwood figured out how it could be done."

"You can't blame Mr. Melville," Robin said. "I've told you that we couldn't raise the imminent danger exception until Stallings was dead. If he was alive, he would have denied confessing. And even after Stallings died, it was a long shot. We were lucky Judge Davies bought it. I can think of a number of judges who wouldn't have."

Jose turned to her. "At least you tried, which is more than I can say for our host."

Jose stood up and looked Melville in the eye.

"I only came here so I could say this to your face. If you're looking for forgiveness, you're wasting your time."

Then he walked out of the room.

Robin stood up and turned to go after Jose, but Melville stopped her. He looked lost.

"Let him go. I knew he might never forgive me, but I hoped . . ."

Melville shook his head and sighed.

"Don't give up," Robin said. "Jose is still adjusting to life outside of death row. He needs time to think."

"You're right."

"Mr. Melville, you wanted Ken to come to Black Oaks, and I understand that it has something to do with Corey Rockwell."

"It does, but I'm not up to discussing it now. Let's meet tomorrow, and I'll tell you what I had in mind."

CHAPTER NINETEEN

Something was off. Rockwell was sure of it. He'd always had a funny feeling about Melville's film project, but he was desperate, and he had rationalized away any misgivings because he needed cash and craved the spotlight again. Melville really had him going until he mentioned Rose McIntire and Tony Clark.

Melville had tried to disguise his interest by concealing what he was really interested in with talk about screenwriters and research. It hadn't worked. Melville showed his hand when he talked about freeing innocent people from prison. Rockwell was certain that Melville thought that Yousef Khan was innocent, and he was going to try to get him out of prison by proving Corey was the killer. That was why he needed to find McIntire and Clark.

Rockwell was sure he was right. But what if he wasn't? What if the movie deal was legit? He couldn't risk being wrong. So, he came up with a plan.

Dinner was at seven. Rockwell went down a little before and waited until Frank Melville, Nelly Melville, Sheila Monroe, and Justin Trent were in the dining hall. That accounted for everyone with a room on the third floor's east wing.

Justin and Nelly walked toward the fireplace, and Frank and Sheila went to one end of the dining room table. Rockwell left the room while they were distracted and raced up the stairs. He paused before he reached the landing and listened for any sign that Lockwood, Alvarez, or Breland were out of their rooms.

He was about to climb the rest of the flight when Lockwood's door opened. He had made up a story about having to go to his room for his phone, but he didn't have to use it, because Lockwood knocked on Alvarez's door. Moments later, she was inside, and Rockwell was sprinting down the hall in the east wing and sneaking into Melville's office.

It was dark in the office, and he didn't want to risk turning on the light, so he used the beam from his cell phone. Melville had taken a thick file from a drawer in the cabinet behind the desk. Rockwell opened the drawer. There were several files in the cabinet, but he had no trouble finding a file with his name on it.

Rockwell opened the file and illuminated the pages. It didn't take him long to figure out that Melville had no interest in making a motion picture. Melville wanted to put him in prison.

Rockwell returned the file to its proper place and opened the office door a crack. When he didn't see anyone in the hall, he walked to the landing and down the stairs. Rockwell paused at the entrance to the dining room. Two waiters were circulating with hors d'oeuvres. When he was certain that no one was looking his way, Rockwell walked over to one of the waiters and took a cracker topped with brie and prosciutto and carried it over to the end of the table where Sheila Monroe and Frank Melville were talking.

CHAPTER TWENTY

Robin went to Jose's room before going down to dinner. She knocked and he told her to come in. Jose had battled boredom on death row by reading. The longer the book, the more time he had with it, so he was attracted to any oversized tome regardless of genre. When Robin walked in, Jose was sitting in an armchair next to the window with a copy of *War and Peace*.

"They're serving dinner," Robin said. "Are you ready to go down?"

Jose put the book in his lap and shook his head.

"I'm not hungry."

"Look, Jose, I understand how you feel about Mr. Melville, but going on a hunger strike isn't going to make him feel any worse than he does already, and the food here is very good."

"I know what you're trying to do, but it won't work. Please make my excuses."

Robin was tempted to try and change Jose's mind,

but she realized that he was now in a position to choose what he wanted to do after thirty years of someone else controlling his every move, so she left the room.

When Robin entered the dining hall, she heard the hum of the wind through the stone walls of the manor house and the *rat-a-tat* of the rain as it beat against the stained-glass windows.

Frank Melville had hired a caterer, and a middle-aged man and a young woman dressed in identical white shirts and black slacks were crisscrossing the cavernous dining hall with trays of hors d'oeuvres. The moment Robin walked into the room, the man approached her, and Robin plucked a stuffed mushroom off his tray.

"Can I get you a cocktail?" the man asked.

"A screwdriver would be great. Go heavy on the orange juice and light on the vodka."

The waiter smiled. "Coming right up."

Robin surveyed the dining hall and saw Nelly Melville talking to a handsome young man near the fireplace on the other side of the room. Their heads were inches apart, and they looked serious.

Sheila Monroe was standing next to Frank Melville at the end of the long dining hall table. Her red dress set off her honey-colored hair, and a colorful shawl was draped across her shoulders. Corey Rockwell completed the trio.

Robin looked toward the door to the kitchen and saw Mrs. Raskin, the person she'd been looking for, talking to one of the other servers. Robin walked over to her.

"Can I ask you a favor, Mrs. Raskin?"

"Of course."

"Mr. Alvarez doesn't want to come down to dinner. Can you check on him in a bit to see if he wants food sent up to his room?"

"I'll go up after the first course is served."

"Thanks."

The server brought Robin her screwdriver just as Mrs. Raskin walked over to Mr. Melville and whispered in his ear. He looked upset. He said something to his housekeeper, and she picked up a place card with Jose's name from a setting and rearranged the table.

"Robin Lockwood?"

Robin turned and came face-to-face with the man who had been talking to Nelly Melville by the fireplace. He was about her age and had the look of someone who played tennis at an exclusive country club. The man's hand-tailored suit fit his athletic body perfectly, and his curly blond hair set off his tan and bright blue eyes. He extended a hand.

"Justin Trent. Nelly told me you'd be coming."

"You're Mr. Melville's lawyer?"

"I am."

"Are you here on business?"

"And pleasure. Mr. Melville invited me in my professional capacity, but the visit gives me a chance to see Nelly."

Nelly Melville had followed Trent. "Do you two know each other?" she asked.

"I don't think we've ever met," Trent said, as he

flashed a smile that displayed perfect, pearl-white teeth. "Civil attorneys and criminal defense attorneys travel in different circles. But Miss Lockwood is famous in all of Oregon's legal circles."

"Infamous is more like it," Robin said to cover her embarrassment.

"I hear things didn't go well when Dad met with Mr. Alvarez," Nelly said.

Robin sobered. "That's an understatement."

"Now that I know that Dad knew Mr. Alvarez was innocent for years and didn't tell anyone, I can see why he would be angry."

"He couldn't tell anyone, Nelly. He was in a terrible bind," Robin said. "Your father was forbidden to reveal what Stallings told him by the attorney-client privilege. Stallings would have denied confessing if Frank forced the issue. Until Stallings died, there was nothing your father could do."

"I get that. Still, he could have made the effort."

"And Jose would have stayed on death row," Robin said.

Nelly shivered. "I can't imagine what it must have been like to spend thirty years in a cell when you knew you were innocent."

"I visit the state pen a lot. It's what keeps me on the straight and narrow," Robin said. "Every time I think about robbing a bank, I imagine what it would be like to be caged at OSP for even one day."

Frank Melville broke off his conversation when he saw Ken Breland walk into the dining room.

"We're all here, so why don't we take our seats."

Frank rolled his chair to the head of the table. Robin had taken Jose's place on Melville's left side, and Sheila Monroe was on Melville's right. Ken Breland was seated next to Sheila, and Corey Rockwell was seated next to Ken. That protected the females in the room from his advances, because Nelly was seated next to Robin, and Justin Trent was across from the actor.

When everyone was seated, Frank Melville raised his glass.

"I want to propose a toast to Robin Lockwood, who used her brilliant legal skills to free Jose Alvarez from death row; a feat I thought was impossible."

"Hear! Hear!" Justin Trent said as the glasses sailed skyward in a salute to Robin.

Robin blushed. "This was a group effort, Mr. Melville. I had incredible help from Ken and Loretta Washington, my associate."

Melville smiled. "Don't be modest, my dear. I can't think of another attorney who could have done what you did."

"Maybe you should show your gratitude by offering Miss Lockwood a part in our movie," Corey Rockwell said.

Robin laughed. "I had my star turn in Las Vegas. Once was enough."

Rockwell flashed a lecherous grin. "If we worked together, you might find a second time in the spotlight rewarding."

Just then, the waiters rescued Robin by placing a hearty vegetable soup in front of the diners.

"I thought this would be appropriate for a night like this," said Nelly, who had created the menu.

"It's perfect," Justin said, gracing Nelly with a smile.

"Has Mr. Alvarez told you what he plans to do, now that he's a free man?" Frank Melville asked.

"No. I asked him about finishing his college degree, but he's in his midfifties. He doubts anyone would hire him."

Melville looked sad. "He's probably right. So, he has no plans?"

"Nothing concrete. But he's just out of prison."

Melville brightened. "We're going to work on this little problem. And I'd like any suggestions anyone can give me, because I am dedicating myself to making the rest of Mr. Alvarez's life the success he would have had if he hadn't suffered this horrible tragedy."

The waiters brought out prime rib, and Corey Rockwell dominated the conversation during the main course with Hollywood gossip. Everyone seemed content to let the actor steal the limelight because his stories were entertaining and a distraction from thinking about the horrors their missing dinner guest had endured.

After everyone had finished the main course, the servers brought out apple pie and coffee. The level of conversation dropped while the diners dug into their dessert, and Frank Melville tapped his fork against his water glass.

"I have an announcement to make," he said. "As you know, Katherine, my dear wife, died in the accident that left me paralyzed. After the crash, I resigned myself to being lonely, never believing that I could find true love again."

Melville took Sheila Monroe's hand. "Then Sheila came into my life, and, like Robin's miracle, the impossible happened."

Melville paused and looked adoringly at his dinner partner.

"I want you to be the first to know that I have asked Sheila to marry me, and she has accepted."

There was stunned silence around the table. Then Rockwell started clapping, and everyone except Justin Trent joined in.

Sheila was about to say something when the sound of the wolf's head door knocker echoed through the mansion. All heads turned in the direction of the entry hall.

"Who could possibly be out in this storm?" Nelly asked, stating what everyone around the table was thinking.

The knocker crashed against the door again, and, moments later, Luther led a middle-aged man into the dining hall. His pale, blue eyes were bloodshot, and rainwater dripped from his long, brown hair and down a face covered in a salt-and-pepper stubble. The man's clothing was soaking wet, and mud stained his sleeves, his knees, and the lower legs of his slacks.

"I'm Carl Samuels," the man said. "I'm a detective with the county sheriff, and I apologize for interrupting your dinner."

"What happened to you?" Frank Melville asked.

"My car slid off of the road and through a guard-rail. Fortunately, a thick tree stopped my descent."

"Are you alright?" Sheila asked.

"The crash shook me up, but I only have a few scrapes and bruises."

"Who should we call?" Frank Melville asked.

"I don't think you'll be able to get a call through. I tried calling for help, but there's no cell service up here."

"You can use our landline."

"I can try, but it wouldn't matter. The road up the mountain is blocked in two places by mudslides. No one can get through until the road is cleared."

"What were you doing driving in this storm?" Justin Trent asked.

Samuels hesitated before answering Trent's question.

"I don't want to alarm you, but Victor Zelko, an inmate at the state hospital, escaped just before the storm broke. I'm part of a group hunting for him."

CHAPTER TWENTY-ONE

Sheila Monroe gasped when she heard the name of the escaped inmate, and everyone looked at her.

"Who is Victor Zelko?" Corey Rockwell asked.

"Zelko is a deranged actor who went on a killing spree," Sheila said. "The press called him the Chameleon because he used a disguise each time he killed. The police didn't figure out that a serial killer was at work for a long time because eyewitnesses gave completely different descriptions of the killer in each case. When a forensic expert found wig hairs and other indications that the killer had been disguising himself, the focus narrowed to a delusional actor who imagined that he had a grudge against the victims."

"Wasn't Zelko found not guilty but insane?" Robin asked.

Sheila nodded. "He was committed to the state hospital. Soon after, he set a fire and escaped. Some inmates and a guard died, but Zelko and two inmates got away. He killed once more before he was recaptured."

"How do you know so much about Zelko?" Samuels asked.

"I researched Zelko's case for Frank because an innocent man was blamed for one of his murders." Sheila looked at Samuels. "How did Zelko escape again? Wasn't he kept in solitary confinement after his last escape?"

"Zelko's very resourceful. He faked an injury. When he was in the infirmary, he killed a doctor and disguised himself so he looked like his victim."

"This is no time to interrogate Detective Samuels," Frank Melville said. "Justin, you're about the same size as Mr. Samuels. Do you have some dry clothes that will fit him?"

"I do." Justin stood up. "Come up to my room, Detective."

"Luther, follow them and take charge of Mr. Samuels's wet clothes," Frank Melville said. "Then tell Mrs. Raskin to prepare a room for our guest."

Frank turned to the detective. "When you're ready, come down and we'll give you dinner."

"Thanks for everything," Samuels said.

Frank smiled. "No need to thank me. Now, go get out of those wet clothes."

Justin and Samuels left the dining hall with Luther in tow.

Nelly stood up. "With your announcement, Dad, and Detective Samuels's dramatic entrance, we've certainly had enough drama for one night. Does anyone want a stiff drink?"

Several of the diners raised their hands. Nelly went into the kitchen with the drink orders, and everyone started talking about the escaped madman. The conversation died down when the woman waiter came out of the kitchen with a tray of drinks. She was handing out the last drink to Corey Rockwell when Justin Trent and Detective Samuels walked into the dining room.

"I tried the landline," Justin Trent said. "It's down."

"I'm not surprised," Sheila said. "This storm is creating havoc."

"You look much better," Frank said to Samuels. "I bet you're starving."

"Some food would be great," Samuels said.

Nelly came out of the kitchen, and Frank told one of the waiters to bring Samuels a meal. No one disturbed Samuels while he ate, and Nelly tried to divert everyone's attention away from the storm and the escaped killer by asking Sheila and her father about their wedding plans.

"You must be exhausted," Frank said when Samuels cleared his plate.

"I could use some sleep," he admitted.

"I think we all could," Frank said.

Melville's wheelchair was motorized, and he maneuvered away from the table and toward the hall. The other guests started walking toward the stairs to the upper floors. Frank had just entered the corridor outside the dining hall when the door from the kitchen opened and the caterers, a man and a woman in their late twenties, and the two waiters, walked into the corridor.

"Mr. Melville," the woman caterer said.

"Yes, Janet?"

"Your daughter told us that the road to town is blocked by mudslides. Is it still impassable?"

Frank turned to Samuels.

"As far as I know, it hasn't been cleared," Samuels said.

"Do you have room for Max and me, and Sandy and Milo?" Janet asked.

"Can we accommodate them?" Frank asked Nelly.

"There are several empty rooms on the second floor," Nelly said. "I'll have Mrs. Raskin take you up."

As if on cue, Mrs. Raskin walked toward them. She was carrying a wooden box, and she looked grim.

"I found this on the table near the front door," she told her employer as she handed Frank Melville a card. "This note was with it. It says it's for you."

Frank Melville's smile disappeared when he saw what was inscribed on the lid, and his hand shook when he opened the box. As soon as he looked inside, Melville turned pale and clutched his chest.

"Frank, what's wrong?" Sheila asked.

"Take Dad to the library," Nelly said as she took the box from her father's hands. Sheila pushed Melville out of the room.

"Who did this?" Nelly demanded.

No one answered her.

Nelly glared at the guests. Then she turned on her

heel and followed her father with Justin Trent behind her.

Before Nelly walked away, Robin had looked at the box. It was engraved with a bloodred pentagram and contained a knife with a silver handle that looked like a claw that was half-human, half-wolf.

CHAPTER TWENTY-TWO

Melville stopped his wheelchair in the middle of the room and took some deep breaths. Sheila draped her shawl across his shoulders for warmth and hovered over him while Nelly walked to the end of the room and set the box on the mantel.

Mrs. Raskin had taken the catering crew to their rooms. Justin Trent, Samuels, and Corey Rockwell circled their host with their backs to the fireplace, and Robin and Ken stood with their backs to the library door.

"Are you okay?" Sheila asked Frank.

Melville shook his head. "The box and that knife . . . It was just a shock."

"It's someone's idea of a sick joke," Nelly said.

"Who could have done it?" Sheila asked.

"Anyone who knows the Black Oaks legend and Frank's fear of the curse," Justin Trent said.

"Which narrows the suspects to everyone in the house," Nelly said.

"Except the caterers," Trent said.

"How do we know they didn't research the Black Oaks legend after they were hired?" Nelly said.

"Who did hire them?" Trent asked.

"Mrs. Raskin," Nelly answered.

"Did she vet them?" Trent asked.

"Emily checked their references. Max and Janet DeNucci's are excellent. They brought Milo Corrigan and Sandy Merrick, the servers, with them, so we didn't do any kind of background check on them."

"I don't think it's likely that our caterers are the culprits," Sheila said.

"Well, someone here is," Justin Trent said.

Justin's brow furrowed. "Where is Alvarez? He wasn't at dinner."

"He's in his room," Robin said.

"You're not suggesting that Jose is responsible, are you?" Frank asked.

"He would have had a golden opportunity to plant the box while everyone was in the dining room."

"No, no," Frank said. "We are not going to accuse that man of anything after what he's gone through."

"Justin, stop it," Nelly said. "You're upsetting Dad."

"I'm sorry," Justin apologized.

"It's getting late," Nelly said. "Why don't all of you get some sleep. Sheila and I will look after my father."

Trent, Samuels, and Rockwell headed for the elevator. Robin, who was still leery of the contraption, took the stairs, and Ken followed her.

"I think Melville is in danger," Robin told Ken.

"I agree, but from whom?"

"Does anything about Rockwell being here seem off? I mean, if I was going to finance a film, why would I want a has-been like Rockwell in the lead? I asked Sheila about the movie deal, and she said there was more to it, but didn't elaborate."

"Melville has been working on cold cases where innocent people were sent to prison for murders they didn't commit. Wasn't Rockwell's wife murdered?" Ken asked.

"I think so. And Melville told me he wanted you to come to Black Oaks because he had more work for us. I wonder if it involves the murder of Rockwell's wife."

"We're not going to find out tonight," Ken said. "We can ask Melville why he wanted me here in the morning."

CHAPTER TWENTY-THREE

Ken said good night and went into his room. It was almost midnight when Robin went into hers. She was tired, but she was too wound up to go to sleep. The appearance of Detective Samuels and the box with the satanic inscription and its eerie contents had been unsettling. And there was something that had happened at dinner that had struck her as odd, but she couldn't remember what it was.

Robin had brought a draft of a brief that was due in the Ninth Circuit Court of Appeals with her. She took it out of her overnight bag, figuring that reviewing it would put her to sleep as effectively as a sleeping pill. She was just starting to feel drowsy when the elevator alarm went off. Robin stopped reading and looked at the clock on her nightstand.

Robin resumed reading the brief, assuming that someone would respond to the alarm, but it didn't stop. Robin got up and went into the hall. A second later,

Corey Rockwell walked out of his room. They both looked down the elevator shaft. Ken walked out of his room, and Justin Trent walked onto the landing from the Melville family wing. Then Jose came out of his room.

"What's going on?" Jose asked.

"I don't know," Robin answered. She looked down the shaft. The elevator looked like it was stuck between the second and third floors.

Nelly Melville ran up the stairs with Sheila close on her heels.

"Dad, Dad!" Nelly yelled.

Robin hesitated. Then she climbed into the shaft, dropped onto the top of the car, and pried open the escape hatch. Frank Melville's head was resting against the back of the wheelchair. His eyes stared at Robin, who had seen enough corpses to know that Melville wasn't seeing anything.

Robin edged down into the narrow space between the wheelchair and the side of the car. When she landed, her foot hit something. She looked down and saw a small piece of rounded pipe rolling across the floor.

Robin reached across Melville to turn off the alarm, and the shawl fell on the floor of the car revealing the front of Melville's shirt. It was stained red with blood, and protruding from the stain was the hilt of the knife that had been in the box with the bloodred pentagram on its cover.

Robin pressed the button for the third floor, and the elevator lurched upward. Nelly ripped open the gate as soon as the car arrived. Robin heard a glass shatter on the stone steps, and Sheila started toward Melville.

Robin edged around the wheelchair and held out her hand to stop Nelly and Sheila from entering the car.

"You can't touch Frank," she said. "The police need to examine him. You'll disturb evidence."

Nelly backed away, but Sheila acted as if she hadn't heard Robin. Robin moved between Sheila and the dead man.

"Please, Sheila. We have to find out who did this. I know what you're going through. I watched my fiancé die too. But you've got to pull yourself together."

Sheila sagged and began to cry. Robin moved her away from the car, and Nelly draped an arm across her shoulder. Justin Trent walked down the stairs and placed a comforting hand on Nelly's arm.

Ken walked down the stairs until he was near the car. Jose and Rockwell stayed on the landing, and Samuels stood behind them. Robin saw Mrs. Raskin, Luther, and the caterers looking up from the second-floor landing.

"Everybody, stand back," Ken commanded. "This is a crime scene. You don't want to contaminate it."

"What do you want to do, Detective?" Robin asked Samuels.

Samuels looked like he hadn't heard Robin, so she repeated her question. Samuels started. Then he looked at Robin.

"Yeah," Samuels said. "Everyone stay out of the elevator. We have to preserve the scene for the boys from the crime lab."

"Maybe, everyone should go down to the library," Ken suggested.

"That's a good idea," Samuels agreed.

Mrs. Raskin, Luther, and the caterers started down the stairs. Ken, Sheila, Jose, and Rockwell followed them, but Nelly stayed behind. Trent looked like he was going to stay too, but Nelly told him to look after Sheila.

"We can't leave my father in the elevator," Nelly said. "Mudslides are blocking the road, and the phones don't work. We don't know when anyone will get here."

"You're right," Robin said. "Is there a room we can put him in?"

"His bedroom," Nelly said.

"That sounds good," Samuels said.

"Do you have a phone, Robin?" Nelly asked. "You can get pictures of the crime scene before we move Dad."

"Good idea," Robin said. "It's in my room."

Robin ran to get the phone. It took her a few minutes to remember where she'd put it. Since there was no cell service on the mountain, she'd left it in her overnight bag. She grabbed the phone and left her room. Samuels was where she'd left him, and Nelly was standing on the landing with Sheila's shawl. Robin took several pictures. Then she pushed the wheelchair onto the landing and took more pictures of the car after the body and wheelchair had been removed.

Nelly and the detective waited until Robin had finished documenting the crime scene. Then Nelly led the way to Melville's bedroom. Robin followed with the wheelchair with Samuels tagging behind. Nelly stood aside, and Robin pushed the dead man inside.

"Help me lift Mr. Melville onto the bed," Robin said.

Samuels grabbed Melville's legs, and Robin lifted Melville's shoulders. While they were maneuvering Melville onto his bed, Robin noticed a circular bruise on the dead man's forehead.

"We better leave the shawl here," Robin told Nelly. "It was over your dad's shoulders, and there might be trace evidence on it."

Nelly laid the shawl on the bed beside the dead man.

"Let's go downstairs," Samuels said. He held the door for Nelly and Robin. Robin started to follow Nelly when something occurred to her. She walked to the bed and stared at the handle of the knife. She circled it with her hands, careful not to touch it.

"Miss Lockwood?" Samuels said.

"Sorry."

Robin walked into the hall, and Samuels closed the door. When they got back to the elevator, Nelly went down the stairs. Samuels started after her, but Robin told him to wait. When Samuels turned around, Robin was frowning and staring at the bars that made up the exterior of the cage.

"Something is off," she said.

"Well, yeah. We got a guy stabbed to death in an elevator with a werewolf knife."

"That's not what I mean. It looks like the knife went right into Mr. Melville's heart, so death was probably instantaneous. Do you see what that means?"

"No."

"I used my hand to get a rough estimate of the width of the knife's handle. I think it's too wide to pass through the bars of the elevator. If I'm right, Melville couldn't have been stabbed by someone outside the cage."

"So?"

"If Melville was killed instantly and his body was leaning away from the control panel, the killer had to have been the one who pressed the Stop/Alarm button."

"That makes sense."

"Don't you see the problem? The car was stopped between the second and third floor. If the killer was in the car, how did he get out?"

PART SIX

DUNGEONS AND DRAGONS

CHAPTER TWENTY-FOUR

When Robin and Samuels walked into the library, Ken was talking to Luther and Mrs. Raskin, Jose was standing by himself in a corner, and the caterers were standing near one of the bookshelves, conferring in hushed voices.

Sheila Monroe was sitting in one of the armchairs that bracketed the fireplace. She was bent forward, and Nelly was comforting her while Justin Trent looked on.

Corey Rockwell was sitting in the other armchair, and he looked frightened. When he saw Samuels, he jumped up.

"Did Zelko kill Melville? Is he in the house?"

Samuels held up his hand. "Calm down, Mr. Rockwell. Right now, you know as much as I do about who murdered Mr. Melville, but it probably isn't Victor Zelko. Zelko wouldn't head up the mountain. He'd be trapped up here. We're pretty certain he headed for the highway."

Robin noticed that the box with the red pentagram was still on the mantel. She walked over to it and used her handkerchief to raise the lid.

"The box is empty," she told Samuels. "So, Mr. Melville was probably killed with the knife that came in it."

"Hopefully, the lab can find some trace evidence in the box or on it," Samuels said. Then he addressed the people in the room.

"Does anyone know the exact time the elevator alarm went off?"

"I do," Robin said. "I looked at the clock on my nightstand when the alarm went off. It was twelve thirty-three."

"Okay," Samuels said. "I need to know where each one of you were at twelve thirty. Let's start with you, Mr. Alvarez."

Alvarez glared at Samuels. "Why?"

"The detective is not out to get you, Jose," Robin said. "He got here during dinner, so he doesn't know anything about you or your background."

"What background?" Samuels asked.

"Jose was convicted of a murder he didn't commit and just got out of OSP after thirty years on death row," Robin explained.

"He hated my father," Nelly said. "He refused to eat with him."

Jose's hands curled into fists. "You're not going to pin another murder I didn't commit on me. I had nothing to do with Melville's death. I was in my room, sleeping, when the alarm went off."

"Can you prove that?" Samuels asked.

"What a stupid question. Who would be in bed with me?"

"Cut it out and act like an adult," Robin said. "Mr. Melville has been murdered. His daughter and fiancée are right here and they're grieving. Detective Samuels is trying to figure out who killed Mr. Melville, and you're not helping matters."

Alvarez looked embarrassed. "I'm sorry." He took a calming breath and looked at Samuels. "The alarm startled me, and it took me a minute to get oriented. I looked at my watch, and it read twelve thirty-four. When the alarm didn't stop, I went onto the landing. Mr. Rockwell and Miss Lockwood saw me come out of my room. That's the best I can do."

"Is that right, Mr. Rockwell?"

Rockwell hesitated. "Mr. Alvarez did come out of his room after I came out of mine."

"Who else was on the landing?"

"Mr. Trent, Mr. Breland, and Miss Lockwood."

Samuels turned to Nelly. "Can you tell me what happened after we left you, Mr. Melville, and Miss Monroe in the library?"

"Sheila and I stayed with my father until he told us that he wanted to go to bed. Dad liked to have a glass of brandy before retiring. He asked me to have Sheila get it, and I told her. Sheila opened the door, and Dad drove his chair into the hallway."

"What time was that?" Samuels asked.

"I didn't look at a watch, but it was shortly before the alarm went off."

"Okay. Go on."

"As soon as we were in the hall, Sheila went into the kitchen for the brandy, and I waited for her. My father drove his chair to the elevator. When I turned around, the elevator was going up. Sheila came out of the kitchen with the brandy, and we were starting to go up the stairs when the alarm went off."

"Does that seem right, Miss Monroe?"

"Yes. I was looking for a book to take up with me when Nelly told me that Frank wanted to go to bed. I opened the door for Frank, and he drove toward the elevator. Nelly reminded me to get his brandy. When I came out of the kitchen, Nelly was waiting for me, and the elevator was going up."

"What happened to the brandy?" Robin asked.

"I had it in my hand when we went up the steps. When . . . When I saw . . . I dropped it."

Robin remembered hearing glass shatter seconds before Sheila tried to get to her fiancé.

"Mrs. Raskin, where were you when the alarm went off?" Samuels asked.

"Luther and I helped the caterers clean up the dining hall. Then we all went up to our rooms," she answered. "I had just gotten into bed when the alarm went off."

"Sandy and I were in our room," Janet said.

"Milo and I were almost asleep too," Max said.

"Does anyone have anything to add?" Samuels asked.

No one spoke up.

"There's nothing any of us can do until the road is

cleared. So, I suggest you lock your doors and try to get some sleep."

Robin was about to leave the room when Sheila touched her arm.

"Please come to my room," Sheila said. "There's something I have to tell you."

CHAPTER TWENTY-FIVE

Robin followed Sheila up the stairs to a room opposite Frank Melville's office. The room was small and had a queen-sized bed, a comfortable armchair, a small wall-mounted television, and a desk on which a computer sat. Sheila shut the door and turned to face Robin.

"How are you doing?" Robin asked, remembering how she felt the day Jeff died.

"I'm numb." Sheila's eyes filled with tears.

Robin sat her down on the bed and put an arm around her shoulder.

"I went through what you're experiencing two years ago. My fiancé was gunned down in front of me. This is going to be very hard for you. If there's anything I can do to help you get through it, please ask. Never feel that you're imposing."

"Thank you, Robin. That's very kind of you."

"No one who hasn't gone through what we have can understand how it feels."

Sheila tried to talk, but she broke down and only managed to nod.

"What did you want to tell me?" Robin asked when Sheila was calmer.

"It's about Corey Rockwell," Sheila said.

"What about him?"

"Besides escorting Jose Alvarez, there was another reason Frank wanted you and Mr. Breland to come to Black Oaks. You know that Frank devoted a great deal of his time since his accident trying to make amends for what happened to Jose by working to free men and women who are imprisoned for crimes they didn't commit."

Robin nodded.

"Corey Rockwell is here because he believes that Frank wanted to finance a film based on the murder of his wife, the actress Claire Winters. That was a pretense.

"A little over ten years ago, Rockwell got a part in a movie in which Claire Winters was starring. Rockwell romanced Winters, and they married soon after the movie wrapped.

"With Winters's help, Rockwell got the lead in *Hard to Kill*. Then Winters was stabbed to death. Her car and her body were found on a beach several miles from the house where she and Rockwell were living. The medical examiner said that she died around eleven o'clock at night.

"Yousef Khan, a homeless man, was living in a tent on the beach. The murder weapon was found in the tent. He said he didn't kill Winters, but there had been some terrorist bombings around that time and anti-Muslim feelings were high. Khan was convicted and sent to prison.

"The studio had only modest expectations for *Hard to Kill,* but the publicity surrounding the murder trial made Rockwell front-page news and helped make his movie a blockbuster."

"My fiancé was a big fan of action movies, and he loved *Hard to Kill.* I remember him giving me some background on Rockwell and the film's success. Rockwell was a suspect, wasn't he?"

Sheila nodded. "The Hollywood gossip columns were rife with rumors that Rockwell and Winters were going to divorce. Rockwell was drinking heavily and using drugs. There had been a few public scenes, and the police had received two domestic violence calls. But the police could never get the evidence they needed to make an arrest because Rockwell had an alibi."

"What was it?"

"Rockwell did a lot of his own stunts, but Tony Clark was Rockwell's stunt double when the stunts were very dangerous. Clark lived in a bungalow complex. Rose McIntire, Clark's neighbor, was a big fan, and Clark invited her over for a drink to meet him. She left around ten.

"One of McIntire's windows faced Clark's living room. The shades were up, and she watched Clark and Rockwell. She swore that both men were in the bungalow at eleven o'clock, which is where the medical examiner put the time of death.

"When the police talked to Clark, he said that he and Rockwell were together from seven until two. But the interesting thing is that a year later Clark came into some money and left town. No one knows where he is."

"And Mr. Melville thought that the money was a payoff?"

"Exactly. Frank wanted to hire you to see if you could break Rockwell's alibi. If Rockwell did kill his wife and he suspected that Frank was onto him, he would have a motive to kill Frank."

"Do you have any reason to believe that Rockwell suspected what Mr. Melville was up to?"

"Early today I was in a meeting that Frank had with Rockwell. He seemed to believe that Frank wanted to make this film. Then Frank asked him about Rose McIntire and Tony Clark. I was watching Rockwell. His demeanor changed."

"So, you think he may have seen through Mr. Melville's ploy?"

"It's just a feeling. I could be wrong."

"Why aren't you telling Detective Samuels about your suspicions?"

Sheila looked frightened. "You know I looked into the Chameleon case because we thought that an innocent man had been convicted for one of Victor Zelko's murders?"

"Yeah, you seemed to know a lot about it."

"While I was researching the case, I saw several pictures of Zelko. The pictures were in old news articles and Zelko had a beard, but Carl Samuels looks a lot like Zelko."

CHAPTER TWENTY-SIX

Robin headed to her room. The elevator car was still on the third floor. Just before Robin passed it, she saw someone moving on the second-floor landing. The car blocked her view. Robin walked back to the stairs and saw a shape disappearing into the hall that was directly below her.

Mrs. Raskin had told Robin that she and Luther lived in rooms under the Melville wing. Samuels and the caterers were also staying in rooms in that wing. Mrs. Raskin had also said that the west wing on the second floor was deserted.

Robin walked down the steps to the second-floor landing. There were no lights in the west wing. Robin stared into the thick shadows, but she didn't see anyone. She walked into the corridor and squinted. Nothing moved. Robin stood still for a few seconds and listened, but the only sound she heard was her own breathing.

There were two doors on her left and two on her right. Robin tried the first door on her left, but it was locked. She tried the door on her right. It was also locked, as was the last door on the left.

Robin crossed the hall and tried the last door. It opened. Robin stared into the room. There were no curtains on the solitary window. The rain was now a steady drizzle, and the clouds had parted. Dim moonlight barely illuminated the room. Robin switched on the light and found herself staring at an empty chamber whose only furnishing was a fireplace that was built into the far wall.

Robin frowned. She was certain that she'd seen someone on this floor. If she had, they were probably in one of the locked rooms, but there was always the possibility that her imagination had played tricks on her.

And what if she had seen someone in the hall? What business was it of hers, anyway? Robin shook her head to clear it. She had things to do tonight, and she had to accomplish them before the sun came up.

Robin went to her room and changed into jeans, a long-sleeve shirt, a sweater, and a hooded jacket. Then she slipped her handgun into the holster attached to her belt and took a flashlight out of her duffel bag.

Robin opened the door an inch to make sure that no one was on the landing. Then she left her room and tapped lightly on Ken's door. Moments later, the door opened and Robin slipped inside.

"What's up?" Ken asked.

"A lot."

Ken listened as Robin related what Sheila Monroe had told her.

"Rockwell would definitely have a motive to kill Melville if he suspected that Melville was trying to prove he killed his wife," Ken said.

"And he does some of his own stunts," Robin added. "He looks like he's going soft, but he could still be athletic enough to climb down to the elevator cage, go through the hatch like I did, and climb back to the landing."

"Do you think Samuels is Zelko?"

"After Sheila told me her suspicions, I remembered a few things about Samuels that didn't seem right. When Melville was killed, you and I stepped in to take charge, but Samuels just stood in back of the people on the landing and looked on like a spectator. I thought that was strange, because a real detective would have taken charge right away. And some of the things he said, like referring to the forensic experts as 'the boys from the crime lab' sounded like lines from a TV cop show.

"Then there was something else that seemed off at dinner. I couldn't remember what was bothering me, until Sheila told me that Samuels could be Zelko. How did we know that Samuels was here?"

"He knocked on the door."

"How did we announce our presence?"

"We used the call box by the gate. But the storm could have disabled it."

"Wouldn't the power have gone out to the house

too, if it knocked out the power that works the call box?"

"I'm not an electrical engineer. I have no idea. And why wouldn't he use the call box?"

"Zelko would want to cut the telephone lines, so no one could call to confirm his identity. If he used the call box, he wouldn't have had the time to cut the wires. If he's Zelko, he would have scaled the wall and cut the wires. If the wires have been cut, there's a good chance there's a homicidal maniac inside Black Oaks. And there's only one way to find out."

CHAPTER TWENTY-SEVEN

Ken and Robin waited until three o'clock when every-one should have been in a deep sleep. Then they stood on the landing listening. When they didn't hear any-one moving around, they went down the stairs and along the hall toward the front door. As they passed the tapestries, Robin saw the hanging with the wolf hunt out of the corner of her eye. She had the unsettling feeling that the wolf was watching her. She paused and looked at the tapestry. The wolf was still staring over its shoulder toward the hunters. Robin took a deep breath and followed Ken to the entry hall.

Ken placed a thick towel between the front door and the jamb so they could get back in without alert-ing anyone. When she walked under the portico, Robin stopped. It wasn't raining anymore, but a stiff wind was pushing the temperature into the low thirties and bend-ing the tops of the trees. Robin hunched her shoulders against the cold and scanned the grounds for any sign of

Zelko. Dark clouds hid the moon and cast the grounds around Black Oaks in deep shadows, making it difficult to see. She tilted her head and listened, but all she heard was the wind whipping through the trees.

"Let's go," Robin said as she stepped from under the portico and circled the mansion. She used the flashlight beam to find the electrical and telephone wires. They were on the side of the house. One set of wires were intact. The others had been cut.

"This is not good," Robin said. Ken looked grim.

Robin headed toward the stone wall.

"Where are you going?" Ken asked.

"I'm going to look for something I hope I don't find," she answered.

Robin slipped on a pair of gloves while she studied the wall for handholds. Then she took a deep breath and started to climb. Ken followed. When they were both on the other side, Robin turned to Ken.

"Climbing the wall was easy. Samuels would have had no trouble getting onto the grounds."

There were no streetlights on the road to Black Oaks, and the light from the moon was so dim that it made the potholed surface almost impossible to see. Robin used the flashlight beam to illuminate the uneven road just as a gust of frigid wind swept up the mountain.

Three-quarters of a mile down from Black Oaks, a massive mound of mud had spilled across the road. Robin played her flashlight over it and stopped the beam on several smeared indentations on the edge near the guardrail.

"Someone scrambled across the mud here, and it looks like they were going up toward Black Oaks instead of down," she said.

"I agree."

"Let's see where they were coming from," Robin said as she made her way across the waist-high mound of mud and rock, trying hard to keep from sinking into it.

An eighth of a mile farther down the road, a section of the guardrail had been ripped apart. The jagged edges were pointing out from the cliff and toward the valley. Robin stopped on the edge of the cliff and sent her beam down into the shadows until it illuminated the trunk of a car.

"Hold the light," she told Ken. "I'm going down."

Ken took the flashlight from Robin and lit the way in front of her. Robin's descent was treacherous. Handholds and toeholds that had seemed solid betrayed her and slid out from under her fingers and feet, sending rocks and soil hurtling down the cliff. She made her way slowly, pausing often, her stomach in a knot, as she barely escaped falls that would have killed or maimed her.

When she was almost at the car, she saw the massive tree trunk that Samuels said had halted the car's descent. The passenger door was wide open, and the headlight beams were not on. The driver would have needed to have his headlights on during the precarious drive up the mountain. Robin guessed that they had been turned off to delay the discovery of the vehicle.

"Play the beam over the car so I can see inside!" she yelled up to Ken.

Ken shone the beam through the rear window. Robin edged around the passenger side of the car and peered into the interior. The passenger seat and the rear seats were empty, but the driver was folded over the steering wheel. He was only wearing his underwear. A pair of jeans and a blue work shirt lay on the floor in front of the passenger seat.

The rear window weakened the light from the flashlight beam, and Robin had to strain to see the driver clearly. She was afraid to lean into the car for fear of falling, but she was pretty sure that the dark stain that covered part of the side of the driver's head was blood, and she thought she saw a bullet wound in the driver's right temple.

"I'm coming up!" she yelled.

Robin edged along the car until she was behind the trunk. Then she let go and turned into the side of the cliff. She was certain that she would slip and fall every inch of the climb up the waterlogged, mud-slick cliffside, and it seemed like hours had passed before Ken grabbed her arm and helped her onto the road. When she was safe, she let her legs dangle over the edge of the cliff while she caught her breath. Then she told Ken what she'd seen in the car.

"I couldn't get far enough inside to be certain how the driver died. If I had to guess, I'd say he was shot in the head. What's important is that the driver was only wearing underwear, and there were clothes that looked like clothing an inmate would wear on the passenger side of the car.

"Changing inside the car after it went over the cliff would have been very difficult. If I'm right, the driver was killed while the car was on the road, then the killer sent the car over the side after he changed clothes. I'm willing to bet that the mud-stained clothes Samuels was wearing when he arrived at Black Oaks would fit the driver perfectly."

"We have to get back to the house before Samuels figures out that we're onto him," Ken said.

"My thought exactly," Robin said as she got to her feet. "Are you armed?"

Ken nodded.

"Then let's go."

CHAPTER TWENTY-EIGHT

Robin and Ken raced back to Black Oaks and scaled the wall. The front door was still wedged open. They took out their guns and inched into the entryway. The house was dark and silent.

"Let me lead the way to Samuels's room and go in first. I've done this before," Ken said. "You back me up."

Robin wasn't afraid to enter Samuels's room first, but she knew that Ken had been a police officer, a Navy SEAL, and a CIA field operative, so she was smart enough to bow to experience.

Ken led the way to Samuels's room. He took hold of the doorknob and turned it slowly. Robin tensed. Ken signaled Robin to stay in the hall as he edged the door inward. Then he squatted to make himself a difficult target before moving into the room and aiming toward the bed as he flipped up the light switch.

The bed was empty, and it didn't look like it had

been slept in. Ken stood up and motioned Robin to come in. There were two places where Samuels could hide.

"Cover the closet," he whispered as he moved to the bathroom door.

Ken stood against the wall and opened the door to the bathroom. Robin aimed her gun at the closet, ready to shoot at the slightest movement. Ken moved into the bathroom.

"It's clear," he said after a minute.

Then he walked to the closet. Samuels wasn't hiding inside.

"Where do you think he's gone?" Robin asked.

"I don't know, but we have to get everyone together and let them know what we've found."

Ken knocked on the doors in the guest wing and brought Jose Alvarez and Corey Rockwell downstairs. Robin rounded up Mrs. Raskin, Luther, and the caterers after going into the Melville wing to rouse Nelly and Sheila.

Ken had advised against using the library as a gathering place. It had only one exit, and Samuels could trap them inside. So, Robin and Ken herded Jose, Sheila, Nelly, Rockwell, Mrs. Raskin, Luther, and the caterers into the dining hall.

"Where's Justin Trent?" Ken asked Robin.

"I have no idea. He wasn't in his room, and it doesn't look like he ever went to bed."

"What about the detective?" Corey Rockwell asked. "Why isn't he here?"

"He's missing too," Robin answered.

"What do you mean?" Rockwell sounded panicky. "How could he and Trent be missing? What happened?"

"Ken and I made a number of very disturbing discoveries tonight," Robin answered. "They've led us to believe that Samuels is really Victor Zelko."

Everyone started talking at once, and Robin had to hold up her hand and shout to be heard.

"Calm down and I'll tell you what we found."

When the noise stopped, Robin explained that the telephone wires had been cut. Then she told everyone about the wrecked car, the dead man inside it, and what she'd deduced from these discoveries.

"My God," Nelly said. "Do you think Zelko murdered Justin?"

"I have no idea," Robin said. "Has anyone seen Trent?"

There was a chorus of "Nos."

"Is Zelko armed?" Sheila asked.

"We have to assume he is," Robin answered. "I couldn't get close enough to be certain, but I think the driver of the car was shot. If he was in law enforcement, he'd have been armed, and we have to assume that Zelko has his weapon."

"What are you going to do?" Corey Rockwell demanded.

"Are there any guns in the house?" Ken asked.

"Dad wouldn't allow them," Nelly said.

"I've got one," Rockwell said.

All eyes turned toward the actor. He looked embarrassed.

"I've got a license. It's for my protection. I can't count the number of times some asshole has challenged me because of my on-screen persona."

"Where is it?" asked Robin, who didn't like a potential murderer being armed.

"In my room."

"I'll escort you upstairs and we'll get it," Ken said.

"Is there anything else in the house that can be used as a weapon?" Robin asked.

"I was in the Army in combat," Max, the male caterer, said. "There are knives in the kitchen. I know how to use them."

"Anyone else who knows how to use a weapon?" Ken asked.

No one spoke up.

"Mr. Rockwell, we'll give your gun to Max, since he was in combat."

"I don't know," Rockwell said.

"Have you ever killed someone?" Ken asked.

"I . . . no."

Robin noticed that Rockwell had hesitated. She knew that Claire Winters had been stabbed to death, and Robin wondered if Rockwell had hesitated because he knew answering in the affirmative would have led to questions he'd rather not answer.

"Don't you think it's a good idea for a trained soldier to have a loaded weapon?" Ken asked the actor.

"Okay," Rockwell said reluctantly.

"We have to find Justin," Nelly said.

"I agree," Robin said, "which means we have to search the house."

"We should do it in teams," Ken said. "We need someone in each team who knows Black Oaks inside and out and someone with a weapon, who knows how to use it.

"Robin, why don't you, Luther, Milo, and Janet search the ground floor? I'll take Mrs. Raskin, Mr. Rockwell, and Nelly and search the second floor.

"Max, Sheila can take you, Sandy, and Jose through the third floor. Does anyone have a problem with what I've proposed?"

No one said anything.

"Okay. Now listen up. We're looking for Justin Trent, but a vicious killer with no conscience may be hiding in Black Oaks. It isn't our job to capture or kill him. That's a job for the authorities. Robin, Max, and I have guns, but we're not going to shoot Zelko unless we have to protect one of you or ourselves. Stick together. If you spot Zelko, back off and give him a chance to escape. Understood?"

The group agreed.

"Okay. Let's get going. Be alert at all times and don't take chances."

CHAPTER TWENTY-NINE

"Okay, Luther," Robin said. "I assume you know every inch of Black Oaks. Where should we look for Justin Trent on this floor?"

Luther thought about Robin's question. She noticed that he didn't seem nervous or panicky like some of the other residents and guests of Black Oaks. In fact, Robin could not remember him displaying any emotion.

"The kitchen or the dining hall are the largest areas on the main floor," Luther answered with a voice that sounded like the words had been dragged across sandpaper. "There's a closet in the entrance hall, but there's no place he could be between the entrance hall and the stairs and elevator. That leaves the library, a bathroom, and several other closets."

"We can see that Zelko isn't in the dining room, so let's start our search in the entrance hall and work toward the back of the house," Robin said.

The search party walked to the entrance hall and looked in the closet. Then Luther led the group to the library. After a thorough search of the library and the rest of the main floor, all that remained was the kitchen.

Most of this replica of the original Black Oaks was a duplicate of the English manor house, but Katherine Melville had made an exception in the kitchen, which was a spotless accumulation of glistening steel appliances; a spacious, smooth granite-topped island; and shiny pots, pans, and utensils. The one thing that did not fit in was the scarred wooden door in a dark corner of the large room. When Robin saw the door, something occurred to her.

"Luther, I was told that Black Oaks is a perfect replica of the original Black Oaks in Sexton, England."

"That is correct."

"Wasn't there a dungeon in the original manor house?"

"Yes."

"Does this Black Oaks have a lower floor?"

Luther nodded.

"I assume that it's no longer used as a dungeon," Robin said.

"It's the wine cellar, the meat locker, and storage," Janet said. "I was in it when I got the wine and provisions for the dinner."

"Let's have a look," Robin said.

Butterflies flitted through Robin's stomach as she studied the door. She leaned against the wall so she wouldn't be a target when it opened.

"Stand back from the entrance," Robin said. Luther, Janet, and Milo got out of the line of fire.

"Okay, Luther. Open the door."

Luther twisted the doorknob and pulled. Robin moved her head forward until she was looking into the cellar. She could see the top of a flight of well-worn wooden steps, but it was pitch black, and she could not see the bottom.

"Are there lights?" she asked.

Luther flipped up a switch on the wall next to the door, and light flooded the staircase and the concrete floor at its bottom. Robin took a deep breath and started down the stairs in a crouch.

On her right was the furnace, discarded furniture, piles of boxes, and several large framed oil paintings. On her left were shelves filled with wine bottles, a steel door, and a floor with traces of blood.

Robin made a quick inspection of the stored items. They were stacked too close together to provide a hiding place. Then she walked to the other side of the cellar, careful to steer clear of the blood, and opened the steel door to the food locker. Icy air greeted her when she stepped inside. Provisions were stacked on floor-to-ceiling shelves along the locker walls, sides of beef hung from hooks in the ceiling, and sprawled on the floor beneath the raw meat was Justin Trent.

CHAPTER THIRTY

Robin sent Luther to tell the other search parties to come to the kitchen. Then she waited at the top of the stairs until everyone arrived.

"What's going on?" Rockwell asked.

"I'll tell you in a minute," Robin said. "Ken, please come with me. Max, stay here and guard the stairs. I don't want Zelko trapping us in the cellar. The rest of you stay with Max."

Robin ignored the shouted questions and led her investigator down to the basement. Ken stopped when he saw the blood. Robin opened the door to the food locker and stood back to let Ken inside.

Trent was lying on his back, his sightless eyes staring at the frost-covered ceiling. Sticking out of his chest was a knife. Ken squatted next to Trent and examined the body.

"From the blood outside the locker, I'd guess Trent was killed outside the locker and dragged inside."

Ken studied Trent's hands.

"There aren't any defensive wounds, so he may have been taken by surprise by someone he trusted."

"Someone he believed was a detective," Robin said.

"The way he was killed is very similar to the way Frank Melville was killed. We have a single thrust into the heart. Quick, efficient, and instantly deadly."

Ken stood up. "Let's get upstairs."

"I think there was something going on between Trent and Nelly," Robin said as they climbed up. "I'm not looking forward to telling her he's dead."

Ken shook his head. "It's going to be rough. Losing a father and a boyfriend in one night."

When Robin and Ken climbed out of the basement, everyone was crowded around the top of the stairs. Ken held up his hand to ward off the questions that started to come.

"Robin and I have more bad news," Ken said. He looked grim. "It's Justin Trent. He's dead."

"What do you mean, Trent's dead?" Rockwell asked with a quivering voice.

It was clear to Robin that the actor was nothing like the tough guys he played in his films.

Nelly stared at Ken as if she had not understood what he said. Then her knees buckled. Sheila Monroe caught her and helped her to a chair. Emily Raskin rushed to fill a glass with water.

Nelly looked shell-shocked. Mrs. Raskin helped her drink some water, and Sheila held her hand. After a few sips, Nelly's eyes focused, and she turned toward Ken.

"What happened?" she asked, her voice barely above a whisper.

"Mr. Trent was stabbed, Nelly," Robin answered. "He would have gone instantly without pain."

Nelly started to sob, and Mrs. Raskin wrapped an arm around her shoulder and let her cry against her chest.

"I don't want anyone going downstairs," Ken said. "The basement is another crime scene, so I'm closing this door to preserve it for the authorities."

Robin realized that Jose hadn't said anything all morning.

"How are you doing?" she asked.

Jose shrugged. "As well as everyone else."

"What do you want the rest of us to do?" Max asked.

"Good question," Ken said. "The sun should be coming up soon. How would you feel about trying to get to a spot where there's cell service and calling the police?"

"I can do that."

"If you can't get through, you can walk down until you meet one of the crews that are trying to clear the road."

"Okay," Max agreed.

"Meanwhile, do you think you can rustle up some food for everyone?"

Max smiled. "That's what caterers do."

"Everyone else should go into the dining room. You'll be safe there until the police arrive."

Robin turned to Nelly.

"Ken and I need to look in Justin's room to see if

there's anything in it that can tell us why he was murdered."

Justin Trent's room looked like a photo shoot that had been staged for *House & Garden* magazine. The pillows on the bed were perfectly spaced, the covers were straight and tight, and the sheets were tucked in. His clothing was either hung up in the closet or neatly folded in a drawer.

"You can tell this guy works in a corporate law firm," Ken said as he wandered around the room.

"Are you implying that criminal defense lawyers aren't neat?"

"I'm sure you're very tidy."

"There's something wrong," Robin said when she'd finished pulling out drawers and checking under the bed.

"What's bothering you?"

"When I talked to Trent at dinner, he said he was at Black Oaks on business. We didn't find a cell phone on his body, and where's his attaché case and laptop?"

"Good question."

"I'll ask everyone if they've seen them. If no one has, it looks like someone searched Trent's room and took anything he had that would tell us why he was here."

PART SEVEN

THE CHAMELEON

CHAPTER THIRTY-ONE

The next morning, as light started to shine through the stained-glass windows, Ken and Robin met Max in the front hall.

"You still have Rockwell's gun?" Ken asked.

Max patted the pocket of his parka. "It's right here where I can get it if I need it."

"Don't hesitate to shoot Zelko if you run into him," Ken said. "He's a stone killer and insane."

"I've been in combat, so the pep talk isn't necessary."

"Good. Is your cell fully charged?"

Max nodded.

"Okay. The sooner the police get here, the better. But we'll be able to send for help once the roads are cleared, so don't take any unnecessary chances. If you're in danger, come back."

"Will do."

"Thanks for doing this," Robin said.

Max smiled, flipped up his hood, and headed out the door.

Robin and Ken went to the dining room, where the other caterers had prepared breakfast.

"Max is on his way, so help should be here soon," Robin said.

"We're probably safe, aren't we?" Corey Rockwell asked Robin. "Zelko must have left Black Oaks sometime during the night, right?"

"He's probably gone," Robin agreed, not because she was completely convinced that Zelko had fled but to calm Rockwell's fears.

"He must be gone," Rockwell insisted, trying to convince himself more than anyone else. "Why would he stay here?"

"Why did he even come here?" Sheila Monroe asked. "The highway made sense. He could get a ride if he was lucky. Coming to Black Oaks makes no sense. There's no place to go once you get here. You're trapped. He'd have to go down eventually. But he did the thing that makes no sense and came up the mountain."

That had not occurred to Robin. Why had Zelko come to Black Oaks?

"Maybe the real Samuels captured Zelko, and they couldn't go down to the highway because of the mudslides," Rockwell said. "Then Zelko killed Samuels and had no place to go except up the mountain."

Robin thought that was a possibility, but Sheila's question had her thinking.

* * *

After breakfast, the caterers cleaned up and stayed in the kitchen. Sheila and Nelly sat at the dining room table and talked in low tones. A fire had been set in the fireplace to fight off the chill. Jose had pulled a chair near it and had escaped into his book. Corey Rockwell fidgeted in his chair. Every once in a while, he would get up and pace around the room. Robin and Ken kept their guns handy and watched for any sign of Victor Zelko.

"Who do you think killed Melville and Trent?" Ken asked Robin.

"Zelko is the most obvious suspect," Robin answered.

"True. But what's his motive?"

Robin thought about that. Then she shrugged.

"I can't think of one. But I don't know if he'd need one. I don't know anything about his case, except for what Sheila told us, but we do know he's insane, so, maybe, he just picks his targets randomly."

"The person who killed Melville had to be able to get in and out of the elevator," Ken said. "Where was Samuels when you walked onto the landing?"

"He came out of his room after I did." Robin's brow furrowed. "If the killer had to get in and out of the cage, that lets Sheila and Nelly out. Sheila was in the kitchen getting Melville's brandy when the elevator went up, and Nelly was in the hall near the library. Plus, Nelly doesn't look like she'd have the strength."

"I've seen the *Hard to Kill* films. Rockwell did some of his stunts. He's going to seed, but I'd bet that he's still strong enough to get into and out of the car."

Robin tried to remember what had happened when the alarm went off.

"I came out of my room when I heard the alarm, and Rockwell came out of his a second later. I didn't go onto the landing as soon as I heard the alarm. I might have waited as much as a minute or two. Rockwell could have gotten into the car, killed Melville, gone into his room, and come out again," Robin said.

"So could Samuels. But what's Rockwell's motive?" Ken asked.

"He'd have one if he figured out that Melville was trying to prove that he killed Claire Winters."

"Jose is in good shape, and he was a rock climber," Ken said.

"But he was in his room when the alarm went off."

"Unless he did what you just said Rockwell could have done; go into the car, commit the murder, and go back to his room before you came out of yours," Ken said. "And Jose has a strong motive to kill Melville."

"But he didn't have any reason to kill Trent," Robin said.

"Who did?"

"No one I can think of," Robin said. Then she stopped because she had just gotten an idea. But before she could work it out Luther entered the dining room.

"The police are here. I've opened the gate for them."

Everyone rushed into the entrance hall. Luther threw open the front door, and Robin saw three cars and a van from the telephone company drive around the final curve and stop in front of Black Oaks. Two of the cars were unmarked, and one displayed the logo of the state police.

The doors to the marked car opened first, and Max and a man in the uniform of a state trooper got out and headed toward the manor house. The officer was tall and heavyset with curly gray hair and a bushy mustache. There were mud stains on his trousers and the sleeves of his jacket. Two other officers got out, but they stayed by the car.

The passenger door of one of the unmarked cars opened quickly and a thin man in a brown disheveled suit, rumpled white shirt, and brown tie jumped out. The knot of his tie was down, and the shirt was unbuttoned at the throat. The man walked toward the front door with quick, jerky steps. Robin could see tired eyes through the lenses of his Coke-bottle glasses, and his hair was as rumpled as his clothes. Robin guessed that he had not slept.

Two men got out of the third car. One was an African American and the other looked Hispanic. They were dressed in jeans and rain gear and looked exhausted.

Ken moved beside Robin at the front door, and Nelly stood behind them. The rest of the people who had spent the night at Black Oaks hung back in the entry hall.

"I'm Sergeant Robert Pine. I'm with the state police," the trooper said.

"I'm Robin Lockwood. I'm an attorney. This is my investigator, Ken Breland, and this is Nelly Melville.

She lives here. Has the road down the mountain been cleared?"

"We broke through, and Mr. DeNucci flagged us down. He told us what's been going on here and how Zelko disabled your phones. We're going to have the line fixed, so we can communicate with headquarters and the state hospital. He also said that two people have been murdered."

"Unfortunately, that's right," Ken said.

The two men from the second unmarked car joined Pine and the thin man in the brown suit at the front door.

"These two gentlemen are detectives from the sheriff's office," Pine said.

"Peter Morales and Frank Carter," the Hispanic detective said.

"Is Zelko here?" the man in the rumpled brown suit interrupted.

"Who are you?" Robin asked.

"Sorry. I'm Dr. Lewis Ashcroft, the director of the state hospital."

"Do you have a picture of Victor Zelko?" Robin asked.

Dr. Ashcroft had an attaché case. He opened it and took a photograph out of a file. Robin examined it. Then she answered Ashcroft.

"Zelko was here. We're not sure if he's left or is hiding somewhere in Black Oaks. He pretended to be a man named Carl Samuels, a detective who'd been in a car accident. He fooled us." Robin pointed toward Sheila. "Miss Monroe had seen old pictures of Zelko and told me she thought Samuels might be Zelko. Ken and I left the grounds and found a car that had crashed through a guardrail about a mile down the road. There was a dead man in it. I think he was shot."

"That was the real Carl Samuels." Pine shook his head. "He was a good man."

"After we found Samuels, Ken and I came back and organized teams to search the house. We didn't find Zelko. There's a good chance he left during the night."

"Lucky for you," Pine said.

"Not so lucky for Miss Melville's father, Frank, and Mr. Melville's attorney, Justin Trent," Ken said. "They're Zelko's two victims."

"I'm sorry for your loss, ma'am," Pine told Nelly.

Nelly nodded, her lips in a grim line.

"We've tried to preserve the murder scenes," Robin told them. "We did move Mr. Melville's body. He was killed in an elevator, and we weren't sure how long it would take for you to get here. The body is in his bedroom. I took pictures of the elevator before he was moved."

"I'm sure you did the best you could under the circumstances," Detective Carter said. "The team from the Oregon State Crime Lab is working at the crash site with the medical examiner. They'll come here as soon as they finish. And we'll get more officers to do a thorough search of Black Oaks to make sure Zelko has gone."

"That will be a relief," Nelly said.

"Why don't you come inside," Robin said.

"Who are these other people?" Pine asked when he was in the entryway.

Robin introduced Sheila, Jose, Mrs. Raskin, Corey Rockwell, and the rest of the caterers. She noticed that Luther was not in the entrance hall.

"Would I be right if I guessed that none of you have had a decent meal since Zelko escaped?" Nelly asked Sergeant Pine.

"You would," Pine said.

"Let's get you coffee and something to eat, while you talk to Robin and Mr. Breland."

Nelly went toward the kitchen with the caterers, and Robin and Ken led the doctor and the policemen down the corridor toward the library. She noticed the men taking in the odd and impressive features of the reconstructed manor house as they followed her.

After they were settled in the library, Max and Janet DeNucci brought the new visitors lunch while Robin told them about being hired to free Jose from death row, the invitation to celebrate his release at the manor house, the history of Black Oaks and its curse, the sudden appearance of the box with the werewolf handle, Melville's murder under impossible circumstances in the cage elevator, the search for Zelko, and the murder of Justin Trent.

"That's some story," Pine said.

"I feel like we're in an Agatha Christie novel," Dr. Ashcroft said.

Detective Morales laughed. "You're right. We've got a spooky mansion, an escaped madman, and a locked-room mystery."

Carter shook his head. "I've been a detective for fifteen years and a cop for five before that, and I've never had a murder in a locked room."

"Thank goodness," Pine said. "I like the ones where there's one suspect, we catch him in the act, and he confesses."

"Amen," Morales said.

"I'd like to see the elevator," Carter said.

Robin led the way up the stairs to the elevator, then stood back when Carter opened the gate. The three policemen looked into the empty car but didn't go inside so as not to contaminate the crime scene. Robin, Ken, and Dr. Ashcroft stood behind them on the landing.

"We left the murder weapon in Mr. Melville," Robin said.

"Do you have any idea who sent the knife?" Carter asked.

"No. But you should be able to find out who made it. It's pretty unusual."

"We'll put someone on it."

"You'll see that the handle is too thick to slide between the bars. That means the killer had to be inside the car when Melville was stabbed."

"How did Zelko get out?" Morales asked. "You said that the car was stuck between the second and third floors when the alarm went off."

"That's the mystery," Robin answered. "When the car stopped between floors the alarm went off, but someone in the car had to hit the Stop/Alarm button because you couldn't reach into the car from the outside while the car was moving. Nelly didn't see anyone on the stairs."

"You got in and out through the escape hatch," Carter said. "Zelko must have gotten out through the hatch too."

"Surely Zelko killed Mr. Melville and Mr. Trent," Dr. Ashcroft said.

"He probably did," Robin replied.

"Do you have doubts?" Carter asked.

"Not really. Ken and I talked about this. I was the first person on the landing after the alarm went off, and I didn't go out right away. So Zelko could have gotten in and out of the car before I left my room. My only problem is that I don't understand why he would kill Melville or Trent."

"Maybe he killed them because he's an insane, homicidal maniac," Pine said.

Robin smiled. "That's one explanation, but Zelko didn't strike me as being a raving loony."

"He's anything but," Dr. Ashcroft said. "Victor Zelko may be insane, but he is also brilliant and a very organized thinker."

"I asked Sheila Monroe if Zelko knew Melville," Robin said. "She's pretty certain that their paths never crossed. And why would he murder Justin Trent?"

"Maybe Trent figured out that Zelko wasn't a detective, and Zelko was afraid Trent would tell everyone," Carter said.

"If Trent thought Zelko was a killer, he wouldn't have gone down to the basement with him."

"Maybe he didn't figure it out until they were in the basement," Morales said.

"That's one explanation." Robin shook her head. "I know Zelko probably killed both men, but my lawyer brain is forcing me to look at other possibilities."

"I'm going with Occam's razor," Carter said.

"When there are multiple solutions to a problem, the simplest solution is usually the correct solution," Robin said.

Carter nodded. "If there is a homicidal maniac on the loose and two murders, the maniac is probably the killer."

Robin frowned. "You're probably right."

"This is giving me a headache," Pine said. "Let's take a look at Mr. Melville."

The three men got out of the elevator, and everyone followed Ken and Robin to Frank Melville's bedroom. The corpse had started to decompose, and a pungent odor stung Robin when she opened the door. She was glad that Nelly had stayed downstairs.

Dr. Ashcroft studied the victim, the murder weapon, and the wound.

"We'll have to wait for the autopsy, but it certainly looks like your theory about the cause of death is correct," he told Robin and Ken.

"Let's let Mr. Melville rest in peace," Pine said. "Can you show us where Mr. Trent was killed?"

CHAPTER THIRTY-TWO

Robin was relieved that the low temperature in the freezer kept Justin Trent's corpse frozen and made the odor of death almost undetectable. It also made everyone uncomfortable, and the men took very little time with Trent.

By the time everyone was back on the ground floor, the medical examiner, some of the technicians from the crime lab, and the officers who were going to help with the search had arrived.

Sergeant Pine ordered the search party into the dining hall. Robin and Ken followed him in.

"Mrs. Raskin, Luther, and Nelly Melville can take teams through the house," Robin said. "They know every place Zelko can hide."

"Will Mrs. Melville be up for this? Having her father and Mr. Trent murdered has to have taken an emotional toll."

"She helped when we searched before. But I'll ask her."

"Who is Luther?" Pine asked. "I don't think I've met him."

Robin frowned. "He's the houseman, and, now that you mention it, I haven't seen him since you arrived. I'll ask Mrs. Raskin to find him."

"Is there anyone else who can lead a search team?" Pine asked.

"Sheila Monroe has been living here, but you'll have to ask her if she knows Black Oaks well enough to help with the search."

"Okay. Get our guides together and we'll get going."

Robin left the dining hall and found Nelly, who was slumped in one of the armchairs in the library. She looked exhausted.

"The police are going to conduct a thorough search of the house. Do you feel up to leading one of the teams?"

Nelly nodded, but Robin got the impression that she'd prefer climbing into bed and sleeping for a week to escape from reality.

Robin squeezed Nelly's shoulder. "Thank you. I'm going to find Mrs. Raskin and Luther to see if they'll take the other teams around the house."

Robin went in search of Mrs. Raskin. She tried the kitchen before climbing to the second floor and knocking on the door to her room.

"Yes?"

"Mrs. Raskin, this is Robin Lockwood. May I come in?"

"One moment, please."

Robin was surprised when the door opened. Mrs. Raskin was always so prim and proper, but her eyes were bloodshot, as if she'd been crying, and her normally well-tended hair looked like it had been straightened in a hurry during the pause between asking for a moment and answering the door.

"Are you okay?" Robin asked.

Mrs. Raskin forced a smile. "I'm fine. It's just all the excitement and poor Mr. Melville . . ." She paused and took a breath. "He's always been so good to me, and to go like that . . . He must have been terrified."

"He's at peace now," Robin said, falling back on a cliché because she couldn't think of anything else to say.

"Did you need me for something?" Mrs. Raskin asked.

"The police are organizing a search party to scour the house for Victor Zelko. We want you and Luther to show the searchers every place Zelko might be hiding. Do you feel up to helping?"

"Certainly."

"Do you know where I can find Luther?"

"Isn't he with everyone else?"

"He's not on the ground floor."

"Then I don't know where he might be," Mrs. Raskin said.

"You met Sergeant Pine?"

Mrs. Raskin nodded.

"He's in charge of the search. Go downstairs and he'll find you a group to lead, while I try to find Luther."

Robin walked to the other wing on the second floor and called out for the missing houseman. She was nervous about being alone, and she kept her gun in her hand. When Luther didn't appear, Robin went downstairs.

"I couldn't find Luther," she told Pine.

"Do you think something happened to him? Could he have run into Zelko?"

"I have no idea why he's missing, but we'll have to search without him."

"Miss Monroe has agreed to go with one of the groups," Pine said. "She says she's learned a lot about the house since she's been living here."

"So, we're set."

Pine started to turn away when Robin remembered something.

"Can you do something for me?" Robin asked.

"Sure, what?"

"After we found Mr. Trent, Ken and I searched his room to see if we could find anything that would suggest a motive for his murder. We didn't, but we also didn't find Trent's cell phone or laptop. Can you ask everyone to look for it?"

"You think it's important?" Pine asked.

"Trent and Melville met after he arrived at Black Oaks. No one else was in the office, so no one knows what they were discussing. There's probably something on Trent's phone or laptop that might give us an idea what they talked about. It's a stretch, but the motive for killing one or both of the men might have something to do with what went on at the meeting, and there might be something on Trent's phone or laptop that can tell us what that was."

"Okay. I'll tell everyone to keep an eye out for a cell phone or a laptop."

Pine paired the officers with a guide. Then Pine, Morales, and Carter joined one of the three groups, and they started the search. Robin went up to the second floor with Mrs. Raskin and four police officers. Luther's absence bothered Robin, and she wondered why the houseman would have disappeared. Had Luther run into Zelko? Robin hoped that wasn't the case. She didn't want to stumble on another murder victim.

While the medical examiner spent time with Frank Melville and Justin Trent and the lab technicians examined the elevator and the basement, the search parties covered every inch of the manor house with no more success than the first group of searchers.

Just before the search was concluded, the medical examiner followed the ambulance carrying the bodies of Frank Melville and Justin Trent down the mountain. The team from the crime lab followed soon after.

"I'm convinced Zelko isn't in Black Oaks," Pine said when the searchers reconvened in the dining hall.

"If he is, he's figured out how to become invisible," Morales said.

Dr. Ashcroft had been waiting for the result of the

search in the dining hall. He approached Sergeant Pine.

"It doesn't appear that Zelko is still at Black Oaks, so I'm going back to the hospital."

"Okay. I'll let you know if there are any developments."

"How about you, Miss Lockwood?" Pine asked.

"It's too late to drive back to Portland." She turned to Jose. "Is it alright if we leave in the morning?"

"Yeah, sure."

"Then Ken, Jose, and I will spend the night. Is that okay, Nelly?"

"Of course, you can stay. I don't know how I would have made it through this ordeal without you."

"Then we'll leave after breakfast."

"Are we free to leave?" Max DeNucci asked.

"The road's been cleared, so you can leave as soon as you give a statement to one of my people."

"We're going to pack up, Miss Melville, if that's okay with you?" Max DeNucci said.

"You've been incredible," Nelly answered. "I'll be sending you a large bonus to show my appreciation."

"Thanks." DeNucci shook his head. "This sure hasn't been anything like our typical catering gig."

Nelly smiled and shook hands with each caterer before they disappeared into the kitchen to gather their equipment.

"Are you planning on following your dad's wishes and financing our film?" Corey Rockwell asked Nelly.

Robin could not believe how inappropriate the question was. Then she remembered who was asking it.

"I think that project died with my father, Mr. Rockwell. I'm sorry that you've been inconvenienced."

"Why don't you take a look at the deal later, when you have some time. Mr. Melville seemed pretty excited about it."

"I'll do that," Nelly said in a way that let Robin know that the project was dead.

"When can I leave?" Rockwell asked Sergeant Pine.

"When you've given your statement."

"My flight doesn't leave until late tomorrow. Looks like I'll have to stay one more night, if that's okay?"

"Of course," Nelly said.

"I'm going to leave some of my men here, in case we're wrong about Zelko," Pine told Nelly while Rockwell was leaving the dining hall.

"Thank you."

As soon as Pine left to organize the protection detail, Nelly turned to Robin.

"Will you and Mr. Breland come up to my father's office? I'd like to talk to you about something my father planned to bring up."

When they got to the second-floor landing, Nelly spotted Luther in the hall with the servants' quarters.

"Where have you been?" Nelly asked. "We searched the house again, and we could have used you on one of the teams."

"I went outside and searched the grounds and the woods. I didn't know that others were searching inside."

"Very well," Nelly said and continued up the stairs. When Nelly was seated behind her father's desk and Ken and Robin were seated across from her, she opened a drawer and pulled out a thick file.

"My father invited you two to Black Oaks to celebrate Jose's release from prison. But Sheila just told me that he had another reason. This is a file he compiled on the murder of Claire Winters, Corey Rockwell's wife. Dad was convinced that Rockwell killed her, and he was going to hire you to try and break his alibi in order to free the man who was sent to prison for Winters's murder. I'd like to hire you to fulfill Dad's wishes. Will you accept the case?"

"Sheila already told me that your father suspected that Rockwell killed his wife, so I know something about the case," Robin said. "I'd like to read the file before I give you an answer."

"Of course. Take it back to Portland. Let me know when you've decided."

Nelly stood. "You must be exhausted. I'll have Mrs. Raskin prepare a light dinner in an hour or so, and I'll let you know when it's ready."

Robin took the file and walked along the corridor to her room.

"Are you interested in taking the case?" Robin asked Ken. "You'd be the one doing the investigation."

"Let me see the file and I'll let you know."

Robin handed Ken the file. She thought Rockwell was obnoxious, but was he a killer? She had faith that Ken would be able to answer that question.

CHAPTER THIRTY-THREE

Robin retired to her room after dinner. She tried to work on the brief she'd brought but she was so exhausted that she put it back in her bag at ten and dropped off to a deep, troubled sleep.

In her nightmare, Robin found herself in a dark tunnel. The air was close and damp, and she had trouble breathing. She had to touch the walls to get her bearings. They were cold and slimy with mold.

It seemed to Robin that she had walked for hours when she heard footsteps and shallow breathing behind her. She stopped to listen. The sounds stopped. She was about to start again when she heard a low growl and claws scraping on stone.

Robin's heart rate sped up. The sounds behind her grew louder. She started running. She came to a turn in the tunnel and she stumbled over something and fell. When she looked down, a corpse soaked in blood stared up at her.

Robin screamed in her dream and jerked up in bed. Her heart was beating wildly. Robin swung her legs over the side of the bed and rested her head in her hands. It took her a moment to realize that she was awake and there was no corpse on the floor of her room and no werewolf following her. But there had been something important in the dream. What was it?

Obviously, the werewolf legend had inspired the dream, and she'd seen more than one bloody corpse in real life, including two at Black Oaks. There had to be something else. She ran through the dream again. There was the werewolf and the corpse and she'd been in a tunnel . . .

Suddenly, Robin was wide awake. Was there a tunnel—or something like a tunnel—in Black Oaks? No one had mentioned one—or had they? It wasn't while she was at Black Oaks. It was in Portland in Loretta's account of the Black Oaks legend. Robin concentrated. There was the dagger, the horror of the wedding night, and . . . That was it!

Robin dressed hurriedly, grabbed her gun and a flashlight, and knocked on Ken's door.

"Get dressed," she said as soon as he opened it.

"What happened?"

"I think I know how Zelko got out of Black Oaks, or where he is if he's still here."

As soon as Ken was dressed, Robin led him down the hall. It took a few minutes to wake Nelly, and she looked bleary-eyed when she opened the door. When she saw Robin, her look morphed from confusion to alarm.

"Has something happened?" Nelly asked.

"Black Oaks is a brick-by-brick copy of the original, right?" Robin asked.

"Yes."

"I had my associate research the history of Black Oaks. She told me that Niles McTavish held orgies and satanic rites in the dungeon and secret passageways of the manor house. Did your mother include the secret passages in this version?"

"Oh my God!" Nelly answered, immediately seeing where Robin was going.

"Where are they?" Robin asked.

"There's one on the second floor in the room where Niles McTavish and his bride spent their wedding night. He used the passage to escape onto the moors after he murdered Alice."

"We have to see if Zelko is hiding there, or if there are signs that he escaped through the passage."

"Let me get dressed and I'll take you to the room."

"Do you have any flashlights?" Ken asked.

"Yes. We keep several around in case there's a power outage."

Nelly dressed. Then she handed Ken a flashlight, took one for herself, and led Robin and Ken to the second floor, where she entered the hall across from the servants' wing. As she did, Robin remembered the person she thought she'd seen walking into that wing and disappearing. Could that have been Zelko?

Nelly stopped in front of the door at the end of the corridor that Robin had entered. Nelly opened it and turned on the light. Robin remembered that there had been no furniture in the room.

"My mother never got around to furnishing the rooms on this wing before she passed," Nelly said, her voice dropping as she thought about her mother.

"Where is the entrance to the passage?" Robin asked.

Nelly walked over to a fireplace with an ornate wood mantel decorated with an elegantly carved forest scene featuring foxes and deer drinking from a stream shaded by overhanging trees. She pressed a knob on a side of the mantel, and a wall that had appeared to be flush with the side of the fireplace opened.

There was no light in the hidden recess. Robin directed her flashlight beam into the opening. It revealed damp stone walls covered in mold and cobwebs. Robin pointed the beam at the floor of the passageway. The dust had been disturbed.

"Where does this lead?" Ken asked.

"The corridor parallels the side of this room until it's almost at the outer wall. Then steps lead down under the house and out to an opening on the edge of the woods near the cliff."

"You stay here," Robin told Nelly. "Ken, come with me."

Robin stepped into the dank interior of the passage. The light from the room that illuminated the area near the entrance grew dimmer as she walked deeper into the gloom.

Robin played her light along the floor and walls.

Cobwebs had been disturbed, and there were scattered footprints in the dust.

"Someone's been in here recently," she told Ken.

The tunnel turned, and they lost the light from the room. Robin saw the stairs that led to the exit near the woods. She walked down them. A tunnel led off to the left. She followed it to the end. That's when she saw the exit to the grounds and the body propped up against the wall.

Robin walked up to the body and played her light over it. Victor Zelko's eyes were staring away from her, and his head was bent at an impossible angle.

Robin started to examine the body when she heard something tumble down the stairs. She turned just as Luther stepped over Ken.

"Sorry, Miss Lockwood. I never wanted to hurt anyone. But I won't go back."

Suddenly, Robin understood why Luther had disappeared when the director of the state mental hospital had arrived at Black Oaks.

"Zelko set a fire when he made his first attempt to escape from the state hospital. Two patients escaped with him. That's how you were injured."

Luther didn't answer. He just moved forward. Robin's gun was in a holster attached to her belt. She was holding the flashlight and wouldn't have time to drop it and draw the gun, so she swung the flashlight at Luther. He swatted it out of her hand and moved in on her.

Robin stepped back, but the wall prevented her from going any farther. She was close to the exit, and there was a good chance that she could make it out of the manor house, where she would have no trouble outrunning Luther. But there was Ken to think about. If she did get away from Luther, he would probably kill Ken. And Robin had no idea what Luther had done to Nelly. Robin decided to see if she could talk Luther into letting her and Ken go.

"You don't have to hurt me or Ken, Luther. You helped capture Zelko. I'll tell everyone. You'll be a hero."

Luther kept coming. He looked sad. Robin knew she would have to use every fighting skill she'd developed if she was going to get herself and Ken out alive.

While she was training as a professional cage fighter, Robin had studied street fighting, where ending a fight as quickly as possible, by any means necessary, was the rule. She knew she'd have one shot at what she planned to do. Luther was huge and powerful. If he landed a blow, the fight would probably be over.

Luther's punch was a looping, overhand right; the punch most commonly thrown by an untrained attacker in a street fight. Robin threw up her left arm to shield her face from the punch as she rushed in, leaped up, and smashed her right elbow into Luther's jaw as she came down. The strike acted the way a hammer blow would, shattering Luther's jaw and stunning him.

With a smooth, practiced motion, Robin threw her arm across Luther's shoulder, pulled his head down, and slammed her knee into his gut, driving his air out. Luther's mouth gaped open, and he fell forward. Robin stepped back and smashed her foot into Luther's head. When he hit the ground, Robin stomped on it.

As soon as Robin was sure that Luther was unconscious, she rushed over to Ken. He moaned, and his eyes opened.

"Are you okay?" she asked.

"I'm not okay, but I am alive, so no complaints. What hit me?"

Robin pointed at Luther, who was sprawled on the stone floor.

"Is he dead?" Ken asked.

"Just unconscious," Robin said.

"Did you . . . ?"

Robin nodded.

"Jesus. That guy is a Mack Truck."

"It wasn't easy."

"Are you okay?"

"My elbow hurts like hell. I may have cracked a bone."

Ken shook his head. "You've got to tell me how you did that."

"I'll tell you later. Right now, we need to tell the police who are watching the house about Luther and Zelko, and get you checked for a concussion. And there's Nelly. She may be hurt."

"You just said that we have to tell the police about Zelko? What about him?"

Robin stepped back so Ken could see Luther and the body propped against the tunnel wall.

"Is that . . . ?"

"Victor Zelko. Luther killed him. The first time

Zelko escaped from the state hospital, two inmates escaped with him. Luther was one of them. That's why Zelko came to Black Oaks. Luther must have told him about the place when they were at the hospital. Zelko thought Luther would be able to hide him until everyone stopped looking for him, but Luther had other plans."

Ken looked confused. "Why would Luther know about Black Oaks?"

"I have an idea, but discussing it can wait."

Robin helped Ken to his feet. He was dizzy and had to stop once, but he made it up to the room where the secret passage started. They saw Nelly as soon as they stepped into the room. She was unconscious but breathing. Robin handed Ken her gun.

"Watch her while I get the police. And shoot to kill if Luther comes through that door."

"That won't be a problem."

CHAPTER THIRTY-FOUR

An hour later, Luther was on his way to the county jail. The medical examiner was looking at Victor Zelko's corpse in the tunnel that led to the woods that the Chameleon had never reached, while the men and women from the Oregon State Crime Lab worked around her.

Ken had a concussion, but he rejected medical advice to go to the hospital. As a former Navy SEAL, this wasn't his first experience with head trauma, and he decided that he could wait until they were in Portland to see a doctor.

Nelly had a head wound that bled a lot and had to be stitched up, but the doctor thought it would be okay if she recuperated at Black Oaks. Sheila Monroe promised to look after her.

Robin, Ken, and Detectives Morales and Carter were in the dining room watching Sergeant Pine give Emily Raskin her Miranda warnings.

Mrs. Raskin sat with her back to the fireplace, her shoulders folded inward and her cheeks tearstained.

"What will happen to my boy?" she asked.

"He'll have to go back to the hospital while he waits for his trial, Mrs. Raskin," Sergeant Pine answered. "He killed a man."

"He killed that monster to protect me."

"Can you explain that?" Pine asked.

"Victor Zelko threatened my Luther. He said he would tell the police that I was hiding Luther if Luther didn't hide him until it was safe to leave. He said the police would put me in jail for harboring a fugitive. Luther killed that monster to protect his mother. Surely that should count for something."

"I'm certain the judge will take that into account," Pine assured her. "But, tell me, did Mr. Melville or Mr. Trent know that Luther was a fugitive?"

Mrs. Raskin looked alarmed. "No, no. He would never hurt Mr. Melville or Mr. Trent."

"How do you know that?"

"He would have told me. He wouldn't keep something like that from me."

"To be clear, your son came to Black Oaks as soon as he escaped from the hospital?"

"Yes."

Mrs. Raskin's eyes lost focus for a moment as she remembered that night.

"It was horrible. He was in such pain." She squeezed her eyes shut in an attempt to block out the awful memory. "His face, it was . . ." She shook her head.

"Didn't the Melvilles or Miss Monroe know he was here?"

"It was very early in the morning. A little after five. Still dark out. They were sleeping. I was preparing breakfast when he came." She shook her head. "My poor boy."

"What did you do?"

"I knew I had to hide him, so I led him to the secret passage in the second-floor room. He was in so much pain. We have a first aid kit. I did what I could. I cleaned and dressed the wound. I was afraid it would get infected, but Luther was lucky. It took time, but it healed. I fed him when I could to keep up his strength." She smiled. "My Luther has always been strong. He endured, and he got better."

"How did you get him the job as houseman?"

"Mr. Gilbert left."

"He was the houseman?"

"Yes."

"Why did he go?"

"I have no idea. One morning, we looked for him, and he was gone. He didn't leave a note or give anyone an explanation."

Robin felt herself go cold, and she saw the policemen look at each other.

"Did Luther do anything to Mr. Gilbert?" Pine asked.

"No, no. They never met."

Pine looked like he was going to pursue this line of questioning for a moment. Then he dropped it.

"So, you asked Mr. Melville to give Luther the job."

"Yes. I'd bought him new clothes when I'd gone to town for supplies. His wounds had healed, and he looked very nice in the suit I'd given him."

Pine looked at Morales and Carter. "Anything you'd like to ask Mrs. Raskin?"

The detectives shook their heads.

"Thank you for being so open with us. Now, I'm going to have a policewoman escort you to our headquarters."

"Will I be able to see my boy?"

"Probably not. You do understand that you're under arrest?"

"Yes, but I don't regret what I've done. My Luther has never been right. He doesn't see the world like you and I do. I had to make him safe."

Robin would have liked to know how far the housekeeper would have gone to protect her son if she discovered that Justin Trent or Frank Melville knew Luther was a fugitive and were going to turn him in, but she decided that was a job for the authorities.

Sergeant Pine signaled a policewoman who had been waiting by the door. She came forward and stood by the housekeeper while Pine handcuffed her.

"Is this necessary, Sergeant Pine?" Mrs. Raskin asked.

"It's procedure, but I made sure the cuffs are loose so they're as comfortable as they can be."

"Thank you."

As soon as Mrs. Raskin was out of the room, Pine's shoulders sagged.

"There are times when I hate this job," he said.

Robin followed the detectives and Sergeant Pine into the library, where Nelly had been waiting with Sheila while the police interrogated her housekeeper.

"What's going to happen to Emily?" Nelly asked Robin.

"She harbored a fugitive. That's against the law. But a good lawyer can probably keep her out of jail."

"Can you represent her?"

"I'm a witness, so I can't. Did you know Luther was Mrs. Raskin's son?"

"No. She just said that she'd known him for a long time. My father wanted to help him once he saw his scars. Dad was very compassionate. Luther always did an excellent job."

"Hadn't you heard about the fire at the state hospital and the escaped inmates?"

"Yes, but a month had passed, and Luther's wounds had healed up by the time Emily introduced him to my father. We never suspected that he'd escaped from the hospital."

"Mrs. Raskin said you had a houseman named Gilbert who disappeared without leaving a note or giving notice. Is he alive? Have you had any contact with him since he left?"

Nelly looked worried. "No. And he never asked for his last check."

"We should have the police conduct a search. It's possible that there's another body buried near Black Oaks."

Nelly shivered. "I hope you're wrong."

"That makes two of us." Robin paused. "There's

something else I wanted to discuss with you. It's about Jose."

"You want to know if I'll help him like my father was going to."

"Exactly. He has no one he can count on, and it's going to be tough for him to find employment."

"I won't know my financial situation until I know the provisions of Dad's will. I will help him, if I'm able."

"Fair enough. And I'm going to try to get him a job, so, hopefully, he can be self-reliant."

"I'll also help Emily, if I can. Can you recommend a good attorney?"

"I'll write you a list and give it to you before I leave. What are you going to do now that you don't have to care for your father?"

"I haven't had time to process the fact that he's gone. My whole world revolved around Dad."

"You can resume your studies."

"I don't know if I have the energy to go back to school."

"Do you have any plans for Black Oaks?"

"That's something else I haven't thought about. I'll probably move out and get a place that's a little smaller," she answered with a smile.

"That would be just about any place," Robin said, returning the smile.

"I guess I'll try to sell it, but I don't know who would buy it if I put it on the market."

"There must be an eccentric millionaire out there who will fall in love with a haunted mansion."

"I doubt it."

Robin yawned. She looked at her phone for the time.

"Wow. The sun is about to come up." She laughed. "I just realized that I've been up most of the night."

"You'll want to get on the road. Normally, I'd have Mrs. Raskin whip up breakfast for you, but you're going to have to settle for whatever I can come up with."

"I'll help you. In addition to you and Sheila, we have Ken, Jose, and Corey Rockwell to feed."

Nelly made a face when Robin mentioned the actor's name, and Robin laughed.

"I guess if there's any silver lining to this awful business, it's that you'll soon be rid of the world's most obnoxious action hero."

PART EIGHT

THE STUNTMAN

CHAPTER THIRTY-FIVE

Three weeks after leaving Black Oaks, Robin ran to McGill's gym. At odd moments since she'd returned to the city, she had thought about how good it was to be back in Portland, where there were no werewolves or escapees from the hospital for the criminally insane—at least that Robin knew of—and the answer to who killed Frank Melville and Justin Trent were puzzles for the police to solve.

Sally Martinez was working the heavy bag when Robin walked into the gym. She invited Robin to spar, but Robin had injured her elbow when she'd smashed Luther Raskin's jaw, and it wasn't completely healed, so she told her friend that she was going to take it easy this morning.

After her workout, Robin bought a latte and a scone. She sipped her coffee as she walked to Barrister, Berman, and Lockwood. After catching up on her emails and reading a draft of a motion to suppress, Robin started reviewing discovery the DA had sent over in an armed robbery case. She was halfway through the reports when the firm's receptionist told her that Nelly Melville was in the reception area.

"It's good to see you," Robin said, flashing a welcoming grin.

Nelly put down the magazine she'd been reading and stood up. She looked sad.

"I was in town for the reading of Dad's will."

Robin's grin faded. "Are you okay?"

"Not really. It was in the law office where Justin used to work."

"Come on back to my office and we'll talk. Do you want some coffee, water?"

"No, I'm good."

Robin led Nelly down a hall to Robin's corner office. On this sunny morning, Robin had a spectacular view of a sailboat floating down the Willamette River, the foothills of the Cascade Range, and Mount Hood's and Mount St. Helens's snowcapped peaks. Nelly showed no interest in the view.

"I hope I'm not prying, but I got the impression that Justin was more than just your dad's attorney as far as you were concerned," Robin said.

Nelly nodded and choked up.

"Sorry," she apologized.

"No need. So, you two were close?"

"We were."

"Going to that office must have been tough, so let's change the subject. What brings you here?"

"There were bequests to the Innocence Project and

some groups that are trying to abolish the death penalty, but I inherited the bulk of Dad's estate. Dad used his money for good. I want to keep his legacy alive."

"Have you thought about helping Jose?"

"I'd like to."

"Your father prepaid for two months at the Jefferson Hotel, so Jose has a place to stay until he can afford an apartment. Maybe you can pay his rent and give him money for food until he finds a job."

"That would be great. Let me know if there is anything else I can do for him."

"I will. Is Sheila still living at Black Oaks?"

"Yes, until she can find a place of her own. Dad would have wanted to take care of her, so I'm going to figure out some way to do it."

Nelly looked down to hide her tears.

"I don't blame her for wanting to put Black Oaks behind her. When Justin was killed . . . Well, I know how she feels, and living at Black Oaks would be a daily reminder of what she's lost. I told her she could stay as long as she wants to."

"She'll appreciate that."

Nelly forced a smile. Then she wiped her eyes and took a deep breath.

"Did you get a chance to look at the Claire Winters file?" Nelly asked when she was back in control of her emotions.

"We did."

"Have you decided to investigate her murder?"

"Ken's been researching the project, and I think he wants to take a stab at it."

"What will you need for a retainer?"

Robin told Nelly.

"I'll send you a check, so you can get started."

"Okay. Have the police made any progress in your dad's and Justin's cases?"

"If they have, they haven't told me."

Nelly remembered something, and she looked sad.

"Remember we talked about our old houseman, Raymond Gilbert?"

"The houseman Luther replaced?"

Nelly nodded. "The police searched the woods around Black Oaks and found him buried in a shallow grave. Sergeant Pine told me that his neck had been broken, so they think Luther was probably to blame."

Robin sighed. "That's another tragic addition to Black Oaks's sad legacy."

Nelly looked at her watch. "It's been great seeing you again, but I'm afraid I have to go. I'm meeting a Realtor. She's going to show me some condos and apartments."

"So, you decided to sell Black Oaks?"

"It's still a crime scene, but I'm going to put it on the market as soon as the sheriff says I can show it."

"Good luck with that," Robin said with a smile.

Nelly laughed. "I'll need it."

As soon as Nelly left, Robin asked Ken to come to her office.

"Nelly Melville was just here, and we're retained to look into the murder of Claire Winters. You read the file. Do you think there's anything there?"

"Maybe. It all depends on whether I can find Tony

Clark, the stuntman, and Rose McIntire, the neighbor who says she saw Clark and Rockwell together all evening, and what they have to say."

"What about Yousef Khan, the homeless man who was convicted of the crime?"

"That looks like a dead end. Khan was living in a tent on the beach. Winters's car was abandoned near the tent, and a bloody knife with Winters's DNA was found hidden in his possessions. He was an alcoholic, and he said he passed out around the time the murder would have been committed. His lawyer was pretty good, but he didn't have much to work with."

"What's your next step?"

"I'm going to find Rose McIntire. What about you?"

"I'm going to contact Yousef Khan's attorney."

CHAPTER THIRTY-SIX

The Winters case had been front-page news, and it was easy to find an old picture of Rose McIntire on the internet. McIntire had been an aspiring actress when Claire Winters was murdered; a slender, attractive woman in her midtwenties with a milk-white complexion and hair the color of her first name.

McIntire had roles with a few lines in some B horror movies before the murder, but she'd been cast in *Hard to Kill II* and *Harder to Kill* after she became part of Corey Rockwell's alibi. Her screen credits ended a few years after the publicity attached to the Winters case died down.

Ken had been able to track down the actress because she still received residuals when the *Hard to Kill* movies were shown on television. A call to the Screen Actors Guild had gotten Ken Rose's address and her married name.

Ken booked a flight that got him into Los Angeles

at five in the afternoon. An hour later, he was parked in front of a condominium with a view of the ocean that must have cost a lot more than the bungalow Rose McIntire was renting on the night Claire Winters was murdered. Of course, Winters had been murdered ten years ago, and a lot can happen in ten years.

Ken rang the doorbell. He heard footsteps and was certain someone was studying him through the peephole. Ken flashed his best smile. Moments later, an older, but still attractive, version of Rose McIntire opened the door. She'd put on a few pounds, but her curves and large breasts would have been the rage in the fifties and early sixties when zaftig women like Marilyn Monroe and Jayne Mansfield were the sex symbols.

"Rose McIntire?" Ken asked.

"Yes?"

Ken handed her his card. When McIntire finished studying it, she looked confused.

"This says you're from Portland, Oregon."

"Yes, ma'am."

"Why do you want to talk to me?"

Ken had decided that he would get a lot more information from the former actress if he told her the little white lie he'd used to get her address.

"I'm representing a client who's producing a pilot with a true-crime theme for a streaming service, and he wants to do a reenactment of an old case that received a lot of publicity. You were a witness in the case, and we'd like to get your input. Do you have a few minutes you could spare?"

"Is this about Corey Rockwell and Claire Winters?"

"Yes, ma'am."

"What's the streaming service?"

McIntire sounded excited, and Ken thought she'd taken the bait. He smiled.

"I'm not at liberty to say, but it is one of the major players."

"Is it Netflix?"

Ken winked. "I can neither confirm nor deny that."

McIntire grinned. "Any chance I could get a part?"

"We're just in the planning stages, but you're a professional actress, so anything can happen."

McIntire frowned. "Why the Winters case? I didn't think there was any mystery about what happened."

"I can't reveal confidential information. Let's just say that there is newly discovered evidence that suggests that the man who was convicted of the murder may be innocent."

"I thought the cops got the right guy, that Arab. He had the knife. Didn't they get him on DNA? DNA doesn't lie."

"Like I said, there's evidence that suggests the man was unjustly convicted."

"You can't be thinking that Corey had anything to do with Winters's death. I know for a fact that Corey couldn't have killed her."

"I'd really appreciate it if you could explain why you think Mr. Rockwell didn't do anything wrong."

"I saw Corey in Tony's house when that bum was murdering his wife. I told the cops everything then. You can get the police reports."

"I've read the reports, but I have a few questions I'd still like to ask you, if you have a few minutes."

"Okay, but it's been years. I don't know how much I'll remember."

McIntire opened the door, and Ken followed her into a spacious living room decorated with a Persian rug and comfortable beige leather furniture. McIntire pointed Ken to a sofa and took the armchair on the other side of a glass-topped coffee table.

"This is some view," Ken said as he looked out at the ocean through a floor-to-ceiling picture window.

McIntire smiled. "Don and I moved in five years ago. We love it."

"Don is your husband?"

McIntire nodded.

"Is he an actor?"

McIntire threw her head back and laughed. "God, no. I left that part of my life behind years ago. When Corey's career went in the toilet, mine followed him down the drain. I'd already gotten an accounting degree as a hedge against an unsuccessful movie career, and I met Don at the firm where I was working."

"I saw you had parts in some of Rockwell's films."

"Corey was very good to me after I helped clear him." She smiled. "I think he was grateful for my testimony, but he also wanted to get in my pants. When I made it clear that wasn't going to happen, I thought he'd forget about getting me a part in *Hard to Kill II,* but he kept his word, and he got me other parts too."

"Had you met Corey before the night his wife was murdered?"

"No, but Tony Clark was a neighbor, and I knew he did Corey's stunts. I'd told him I was a big fan, and he introduced us the night Claire was killed."

"Mrs. Winters was murdered around eleven that evening. You said you saw Mr. Rockwell in Clark's home at eleven. How were you so sure about the time?"

"Tony invited me over for a drink around nine. We talked for about an hour. Then Tony said that he and Corey needed to discuss a scene they were shooting, so I left. But I could see them talking. Tony's place was right across from my living room."

"You saw them all during the time Mrs. Winters was killed?"

McIntire smiled. "I wasn't spying on them, but I had a bit of a crush on Corey, so I looked across from time to time while I was watching TV."

Ken had developed a theory, and he wanted to test it out.

"Could you see both men together every time you looked?"

McIntire started to answer. Then she stopped and thought.

"I'm not sure. I saw them both, but the window was small. I'm sure they were both there, though. Corey has black hair and Tony's hair is red, and I saw them both when I looked."

"Together?" Ken repeated.

McIntire hesitated. She stared at the waves invading the beach across the street for a few moments before answering.

"It's been too long, so I can't say. I thought I saw them together, but it's been ten years."

"I'd like to talk to Mr. Clark. Do you know where he lives?"

"Actually, I do. Don and I vacationed in Cabo San Lucas a year ago. Tony told me that he liked to vacation in Santa Maria de la Mar, a little town on the coast. On a couple of occasions, he said he'd like to retire there and open a bar. I checked it out, and he was there. He looked great. Don and I ate at the place. Great empanadas."

"Thanks. You've been very helpful."

"My pleasure. Say, can you let me know what happens with the project?"

"Definitely. And I'll drop a hint about a cameo if it gets green-lighted."

Rose McIntire closed the door and got her phone. Don was in San Diego on business, but he was probably back at his hotel by now.

"You'll never guess what just happened," she said excitedly when her husband answered, and she proceeded to tell him about the Netflix pilot and the possibility of a role in it. Don tried to calm down Rose by pointing out that the project seemed to be in the early stages of development.

"You were around the movie business long enough to know that there's almost no chance the show will get made," Don said.

"Boy, are you a doubting Thomas. Just for that, I'm not bringing you to the premiere."

Don laughed. "If there is a premiere, I'll take you in a limo."

They talked some more, then kissed good night. Rose disconnected and was about to put down the phone when she got an idea. The investigator said he wanted to talk to Tony Clark, and she'd told him where Tony was living. She didn't want Tony to be surprised, so she dialed his number in Mexico to give him a heads-up about being featured on Netflix.

CHAPTER THIRTY-SEVEN

The morning after he flew to LA, Ken Breland called and told Robin about his conversation with Rose Mc-Intire and his plans to fly to Mexico. When Ken hung up, Robin paged through her file in the Winters case until she found the name and phone number for the attorney who had represented Yousef Khan.

"Mr. Dowd, I'm an attorney in Portland, Oregon, and I'd like to pick your brain about an old case you handled about ten years ago," Robin said when Dowd's secretary connected Robin to her boss.

"What's the case?" Peter Dowd asked.

"It was a murder case. The victim was the actress, Claire Winters. You represented Yousef Khan."

Dowd laughed. "I'd remember that case, even if I had Alzheimer's. What's your interest in it?"

"My client has been investigating cases of prisoners who were convicted of murder, but who might be innocent, and my firm has been asked to look into Mr. Khan's case."

Dowd laughed again. "You're wasting your time, Miss Lockwood. There's no doubt, reasonable or otherwise, about Yousef's guilt. The State's case was airtight."

"You're probably right, but I'd appreciate it if you could tell me anything that might have made you think that your client might have been innocent."

There was silence on the line for a few seconds. Then Dowd spoke.

"Okay. Now this is a stretch, but, playing devil's advocate, Yousef never denied killing Winters, but he never confessed either. When I started representing him, Yousef was really messed up. He was homeless, using drugs and drinking anything he could get his hands on. He claimed that he'd been out cold during the time Winters was murdered. The cops thought that was bullshit, but I had him examined by a psychiatrist, and he said it was plausible, given his addiction to drugs and booze.

"Also, Yousef never struck me as the violent type. He went through detox in jail, and it wasn't pretty. Once we weaned him off the booze and drugs, he was pretty passive."

"What about the knife?" Robin asked.

"Yeah, that was the killer. Pardon the pun. It was terrifying; long, wide, and with a serrated blade. Right out of a horror movie. There was blood on the blade and the tests proved conclusively that it was Claire Winters's."

"What did Yousef say about that?"

"He said he'd never seen it and had no idea how it got in his tent."

"So, it could have been planted while Yousef was passed out?"

"Yeah. That's what I argued."

"Can you think of anything else?"

"No."

"If you do, can you call me?"

"Sure."

"One more thing. I'd like to talk to Yousef. Can you ask him if he'll meet with me?"

Dowd told Robin he'd talk to Khan, and Robin hung up. She started paging through a draft of a memo she'd been working on. She was halfway through when her secretary let her know that Jose Alvarez was in reception.

Robin walked down the hall and greeted Jose with a big smile.

"You look great," she said. And he did.

Robin had assigned Loretta Washington the job of helping Jose acquire a wardrobe and an apartment. Loretta was impossible to dislike. After some initial resistance, Jose had put himself in the associate's hands. Giving Loretta the job had paid off, and Jose looked very handsome in a long-sleeve navy blue shirt, a gray sweater, tan slacks, and shined brown shoes.

"Do you have a few minutes?" Jose asked.

"For you, always. Come on back to my office."

"What's up?" Robin asked when they were seated.

Jose looked nervous. "I've been doing a lot of thinking."

Robin smiled. "That's good," she said, hoping that her little joke would help Jose relax, but it didn't work. He looked sad and couldn't look Robin in the eye.

"I was a total jerk when we went to Black Oaks. I should never have treated Frank Melville the way I did."

Jose took a breath before continuing.

"I was so angry that I didn't listen to what you said. Now that I've had time to think, I can see that Mr. Melville truly believed that I killed Margo when he prosecuted me, and I understand that there was nothing he could do to help me until Stallings died. I just wish I could go back in time to when he was alive. It's killing me that he's dead, and I can never thank him for all he did for me."

"Don't beat yourself up like this. Mr. Melville didn't need your thanks. He understood why you were angry, and he accepted it. All he wanted to do was to set you free. Getting you off death row and out of prison made him very happy. If you really want to thank him, take charge of your life and turn the rest of it into a success."

"That's the reason I'm here. I've decided that the best way I can honor Mr. Melville's memory is to go back to school and earn a degree I can use to help free wrongly convicted people. I've been looking at the courses you need to have to be a paralegal, and I want to volunteer at one of the places you mentioned, like the Innocence Project."

"I think that's a great idea. Let me talk to some people I know. Maybe I can wrangle you a paid position."

"Thanks, Robin." Jose stood up and looked at the papers spread over his lawyer's desk. "I don't want to take up any more of your time."

"You're always welcome here. I'll let you know if I come up with anything, and you make sure to do the same."

The door closed behind Jose, and Robin leaned back in her chair and smiled. Most of the time, criminal defense attorneys dealt with the bodies of dead children, battered adults, and psychopaths who didn't feel a bit of remorse for the horrors they inflicted on innocent people and others who whined about how unfair life was. But, every once in a while, a criminal defense attorney did something that made the world better. Freeing an innocent man from a life behind bars was one of those things, especially when there was a good chance that the person you saved was going to turn his life around.

CHAPTER THIRTY-EIGHT

Peter Dowd contacted Robin a week after she called to tell her that his client had agreed to meet with her at the penitentiary and had given him permission to send her his files in Yousef's case. Robin asked Dowd if he would accompany her to the penitentiary to smooth the way for her meeting with Khan. She said she would compensate Dowd for his time, and Dowd agreed.

As soon as Robin landed in Los Angeles, she took a Lyft to a part of LA that had seen better days and walked up to the third floor of a low-rise, brick office building that fit in beautifully in the ungentrified landscape. Dowd's one-person shop was as unimpressive as the attorney, who was in his late fifties, overweight, growing bald, and looked to be a candidate for an early heart attack. The good news was that Dowd had been pleasant when they'd met and had showed no signs that he resented Robin second-guessing the way he had handled Yousef Khan's case. Dowd intimated, with a wink and a nod, that he chalked up Robin's diligence to an interest in collecting as big a fee as possible. Robin didn't try to disabuse him of this notion.

The prison where Yousef Khan had been sent to spend the rest of his life was depressingly similar to every other prison Robin had visited. There were high, thick walls, gun towers, barbed wire, serious and suspicious guards, and steel bars that opened and shut with a dull clang that reminded those men and women who had been convicted of murder that once inside, they were inside for good.

"Yousef is going to surprise you," Dowd said as they waited on one side of a metal table for the guards to bring Khan to them.

"How so?" Robin asked.

"He was a homeless alcoholic when he was arrested. Really sick and thin as a rail. Prison probably saved his life."

Before he could say more, a door opened and a handsome man with the bulging muscles of a bodybuilder walked into the room. Khan was clean shaven with high cheekbones, coffee-colored skin, and bright blue eyes. If she'd met him in Hollywood, she would have guessed he was a star of romantic movies.

Khan spotted Dowd and smiled.

"Hey, Peter, how are you doing?" he asked in a deep voice that had a trace of a Middle Eastern accent.

"Doing good, Yousef. And you're looking well. This is Robin Lockwood, the lawyer I told you about.

She's flown down from Portland, Oregon. I'll let her tell you why."

Robin knew that physical contact wasn't allowed, so she didn't try to shake Yousef's hand. Instead, she nodded and smiled.

"Thanks for agreeing to see me."

"Peter said you might be able to get me out of here. That was a strong inducement to let you visit."

Robin was surprised at how intelligent Yousef seemed.

"Why don't you tell me a little about yourself. Then I'll tell you what I'm doing."

Yousef laughed. "As you can see, I'm a prisoner serving a life sentence, so, unless you want me to tell you my daily routine, there's not much to tell."

Robin leaned toward Khan. "If I'm going to help you, you have to help me. No jokes, just real answers to my serious questions. You haven't always been a prisoner, and you weren't always homeless. Tell me what your life was like before you fell on hard times."

Khan sobered. He looked torn.

"This can't be easy, Yousef, and I'm not promising a thing. Getting you out of here will be very difficult, and there's a good chance I'll fail, but I will only succeed if I have all the information I need."

Khan took a deep breath. He looked very sad.

"I was a history professor in Lebanon. Then the civil wars started. My wife and daughter were killed by a suicide bomber. It destroyed me. For a long time, I lost the will to live. Then I made up my mind that I would die from despair if I didn't get away from that place.

"Eventually, I found my way to California. Unfortunately, I didn't come legally, and there weren't any job openings for college professors who were illegal immigrants. To make a long story short, I became homeless, developed an overdependence on alcohol and drugs, and had the misfortune to be passed out on the beach where Claire Winters was murdered.

"The bad news is that I'm stuck here for life unless you can figure out some way to get me out. The good news is that you get three meals a day and a place to sleep in prison, and they don't let you drink liquor or take drugs. I went cold turkey and got my health back. But I'm ready to leave, anytime you say."

Robin felt awful by the time Yousef finished his tale, but trial attorneys learn to hide their emotions, and Robin did a masterful job of concealing her distress.

"I'm sorry about your wife and daughter," she said.

"Thank you."

"And I'm glad that there's been a silver lining—if a thin one—in your sentence."

Yousef smiled.

"Tell me about the knife. I understand that there's no question that it's the murder weapon and that it was found in your belongings in your tent."

"I did not kill Claire Winters, and I have no idea how the knife got into my tent. That's because I was passed out. I'd drunk myself into oblivion and helped the booze by using drugs. An elephant could have come into my tent and I wouldn't have noticed."

"Thank you for meeting with me. My next step is to read the files from your case and the transcript of the trial. Meanwhile, my investigator is running down witnesses we hope will break the alibi of the person who may have framed you."

"I don't think you'll succeed," Yousef said, "but I'm grateful that you're trying."

Robin let the guard know that they were through. Another guard took Yousef back to his cell.

"What do you think?" Dowd asked when they were heading back to the parking lot.

"I think I have a really difficult task ahead of me."

CHAPTER THIRTY-NINE

The Mexican coastal town of Santa Maria de la Mar's proximity to the sea and inexpensive real estate had attracted a small ex-pat community of retirees interested in scuba diving, parasailing, bike trips, and other outdoor activities. The locals were supported by the ex-pats and the occasional tourist.

Ken's plan didn't depend on Rose McIntire calling Tony Clark, but it would have a better chance of succeeding if Clark knew he was coming. He arrived an hour before sunset and found a sand-colored motel a block from the beach. It had ten rooms that were fronted by a parking lot decorated with empty beer cans and trash. Ken asked for the room at the end. The clerk had no trouble granting his request, since only two other rooms were occupied.

Ken dumped his duffel bag on the bed and was rewarded by a spring serenade. The other furnishings were a scarred, wooden dresser on which sat a television that might or might not receive color images, a chair Ken was hesitant to sit in for fear that it would collapse, and a floor lamp with a low-watt bulb.

Robin's investigator could use a sniper rifle, knives, and handguns, but his favorite weapon was a blackjack; a heavy, flexible leather pouch filled with lead. Ken slipped a homemade blackjack into his pocket in case his plan worked the way he hoped it would. Then he walked down the beach to Tony's Bar.

The bar in Tony's place was on one side of a large open patio filled with picnic tables and had a view of the beach. Two young women wearing jeans and T-shirts advertising the establishment were serving mojitos and margaritas to ex-pats and locals who were devouring empanadas, tacos, and heaping portions of guacamole.

Tony Clark was tending bar, and Ken sized him up as he took a stool at one end. Clark hadn't worked as a stuntman for almost a decade, but he looked like he could step in on a moment's notice. There were streaks of gray in his red hair, but he was as solid as a brick.

"What can I get you?" Clark asked with a smile.

"Rose McIntire told me that you serve great empanadas."

"You know Rose?"

"We just met. I'm doing legwork for an independent producer who wants to make a true-crime series. The pilot is going to feature the Claire Winters murder. Would you have some time to talk about the case?"

"That case is old news, and it's been solved. Why would anyone be interested?"

"There's new evidence that suggests that the man who was convicted for the crime may be innocent."

Clark laughed. "That's bullshit. They got him dead to rights."

"Perhaps, but you might be able to help round out the story."

"I'm afraid I can't help you. I'm pretty busy."

"We don't have to talk now. Tomorrow would work."

"Not for me. As far as I'm concerned, the police got the right guy."

"The new evidence concerns Corey Rockwell. Did he give you the money to buy this bar?"

"If he did, it's none of your business. And the police know that I was with Corey during the time Claire was killed. So, there's nothing to talk about."

"Not even the wig?" Ken asked.

"What wig?"

"I talked with Carlos Pineda and Irving Ross, the directors on Corey Rockwell's movies where you did the stunts. They both said you wore a wig because of the difference in the color of your hair."

"So?"

"Rose said she saw you and Rockwell in your place around eleven, but she was only looking from time to time through her window into your window, and she can't swear she saw the two of you together at any time. If Rockwell snuck out and murdered his wife, you could have walked back and forth in front of the window and put the wig on and off, so it looked like two men were in your house at eleven."

"Interesting theory, but one you can't prove," Clark said.

"This series will generate a lot of heat, and I'm going to dig deep to find the truth," Ken said.

Clark straightened up. "It's been nice talking to you. If you're interested in empanadas and a mojito, I'll continue our talk. Otherwise, we have nothing to discuss."

The food and drink were as good as Rose had said they were. It was dark when Ken finished eating, and he walked back to his motel along a beach illuminated by moonlight and the occasional glow from a seaside home or business.

It was easy for Ken to spot the two men who followed him from Tony's place even though they tried to be inconspicuous. He'd seen them talking to Clark at one end of the bar while he was eating. Both were large and heavyset, and they looked like brawlers.

As soon as he was in his room, Ken turned on the light and peeked through a gap between the curtain and the window frame. One of the men was in the motel office talking to the clerk. The other man waited outside. Ken waited twenty minutes and turned off the light in his room. As soon as his lights went off, the men walked toward his room.

Ken waited behind his door. The knob turned and stopped when it was clear that the door was locked. Ken heard the sound of a key being inserted and guessed that the men had either bribed or threatened the clerk.

The door opened slowly. A hand holding a knife appeared. Ken snapped the blackjack against the wrist. Bones broke, and the knife fell to the floor. Ken's victim howled, gripped his wrist, and staggered into the room.

Ken stepped forward and snapped the blackjack against the second man's nose. The pain was blinding, and his knife fell when he brought both of his hands to his face. Ken broke both men's right kneecaps, bringing them to the floor before turning on the TV and turning up the volume to drown out the screams and groans. Then he zip-tied the men's hands, made a call on his phone, and began interrogating his visitors.

CHAPTER FORTY

Fifteen years ago, three idiots got the bright idea of kidnapping four girls from an exclusive private girls' school in Mexico City and holding them for ransom. One of the girls was the fourteen-year-old daughter of a high-ranking official at the American Embassy. Another was the fifteen-year-old daughter of a member of the Mexican Federal Police.

Ken Breland led the rescue team. When the smoke cleared, the gene pool was minus three idiots, and four frightened but unharmed girls went home to their families. Ken had handed over the daughter of the Mexican police officer personally. Over the years, they had met for dinner or coffee and had assisted each other when possible.

That explained why Ken was sitting in a comfortable chair in an abandoned warehouse, and Tony Clark, clad only in his underpants, was duct-taped to an uncomfortable chair across from him, while several large men dressed in camouflage and wearing ski masks watched from the shadows.

Clark had been injected with a tranquilizer before being dumped in a van and driven to the warehouse. He had a split lip and a black eye but was otherwise unharmed. Ken waited patiently for Clark to regain consciousness. When Clark was fully awake, Ken smiled at him.

"How are you feeling, Tony? Do you need some aspirin?"

The light in the warehouse was dim, and Clark's eyes took time to focus. Clark stared at Ken. When he figured out who had asked the question, he said, "Fuck you, you motherfucking bastard. Let me out of here or I'll come for you and make you wish you were dead."

"I can understand why you're angry," Ken answered calmly. "But, if you think about it, I'm certain that you'll agree that I'm the one who should be mad."

Ken nodded, and one of the Mexican police officers shined a light on the two men who had invaded Ken's motel room. They were lying on the concrete floor and writhing in agony. Gags stifled their cries. Clark saw the men and began to look less confident.

"I know you sent these two morons to beat me up, because they've confessed. You can see that your buddies are in a lot of pain, but why, you must wonder, are they still alive. The answer is simple. If I'd killed them, they wouldn't be able to provide proof that you are guilty of several serious felonies that could put you in a Mexican prison for a long, long time.

"But all is not lost. You can save yourself. Want to know how?"

Clark glared at Ken, but it was obvious that the investigator had Clark's attention.

"I think Corey Rockwell killed his wife, and you provided him with an alibi. There's no other explanation for why you'd send these two bozos to frighten me. Tell the DA in LA the truth and you'll be able to cut a deal that will send you to a nice American prison for a lot less time than you'll be spending here. Keep being a tough guy and you'll learn what happens to gringos in a prison south of the border."

Ken stood up. "I'm going to let you think about what you want to do. I'll check back with you in a while. By the way, the empanadas were as good as Rose said they'd be."

PART NINE

AN INGENIOUS PLAN

CHAPTER FORTY-ONE

Robin was in the middle of a two-week, multi-defendant, federal drug conspiracy trial, and she was exhausted when she returned to her office at six o'clock. She was organizing the files for the next day's session when Ken Breland stepped into her office and flashed a big grin.

"What's making you so happy?" Robin asked.

"While you were in court, I got a call from the prosecutor who's handling the Claire Winters case. He indicted Rockwell, and your favorite action hero is in jail."

"What about Yousef Khan?"

"His attorney is going to court to get him out of prison, and the DA is going to support the petition."

"That's great news. Have you told Nelly?"

"No. I thought you'd want to do that."

"I don't have time now. I'm meeting an expert witness in an hour, and I've got to prep for the meeting."

Robin leaned back in her chair and fixed Ken with a hard stare.

"You probably wouldn't have been able to get Clark to talk if he hadn't sent those men after you," she said.

Ken shrugged. "Rockwell's scheme took a lot of planning, and we needed luck to unravel it."

"It wasn't entirely luck, was it?"

"What are you suggesting?"

"You set up Clark, didn't you?"

"Moi?" answered Ken, trying his hardest to look angelic.

"You were hoping he'd come after you, so you could use your Mexican friend to apply pressure."

"That would be entrapment," Ken answered with an innocent smile.

"And you would never resort to underhanded tactics like that."

"Of course not."

"Right."

Ken laughed. "I'll let you prep for your expert."

Ken left. When Robin finished her prep, she left for the hotel where her out-of-town expert was staying. As she walked, she had the feeling that something Ken had said was important, but she couldn't remember what it was or why it was important.

Robin met the expert at his hotel and discussed his testimony over dinner. She got home a little after nine and watched the last quarter of a Trail Blazers basketball game before getting into bed. She tried to sleep, but she was still nagged by the thought that Ken had said something important. She tried to block out the thought by thinking about her plan for court the next day. And that's when it hit her.

Robin sat up in bed, wide awake. The word *plan* had triggered the solution. Ken had told her that Corey Rockwell had devised a clever plan. Robin followed her train of thought to its destination. She felt sick because she knew who had the time to develop an ingenious plan. It was the only person who could have killed Nelly's father and Justin Trent. What she couldn't figure out was why the murders had been committed.

There was no way she was going to get back to sleep, so Robin walked into her living room. She sighed. She was going to be a wreck when court started. Fortunately, her expert would take up a good part of the morning, and she had all of his direct testimony blocked out.

Robin stared at the apartments across the way. She assumed that the residents were good people. From experience, she knew that good people could commit the most horrible crimes under the right circumstances and with the right motive. What had motivated a decent human being to murder two people? The answer eluded her for a while. Then she thought she'd figured it out, but she hoped she was wrong.

Robin had to be in court and didn't have time to go to the office, so she phoned Loretta Washington as soon as the sun rose. Loretta sounded groggy when she answered.

"Did I wake you?" Robin asked.

"No. I was just making breakfast. What's up?"

"You have a friend at Justin Trent's law office, right?"

"Yeah. She gave me the background on Frank Melville."

"Do you think she'd give you information about one of the firm's lawyers?"

"What kind of information?" Loretta asked.

"I want to know what area of law Justin Trent specialized in."

"That shouldn't be a problem."

"I also need to know why he was at Black Oaks when Frank Melville was murdered."

When Loretta answered, Robin could tell that she was uncomfortable.

"Wouldn't that involve confidential communications?"

"It could."

"I'm not going to ask her to violate the attorney-client privilege, the code of ethics, and her duty to her firm."

"Not even if it could help solve two murders?"

Loretta was waiting for Robin when Robin got back from court. Robin could see that her associate was upset.

"Don't ever ask me to do something like this again," Loretta said.

"I'm really sorry that I put you in this situation, but you can see why I had to."

"Not really. There had to be some other way you could have found out."

"We talked about that. Have you come up with another way?"

"No. If I had, I wouldn't have approached my friend. And don't ask me for her name."

"I don't need the name, but I do need to know if she confirmed my suspicions."

"She did."

"Shit."

Loretta looked surprised. "I thought you'd be happy."

"I'm not happy at all."

CHAPTER FORTY-TWO

The sun was out, and puffy white clouds floated through the sky when Robin drove from Portland to her meeting with Sergeant Pine and Detectives Carter and Morales, but the sunny spring weather did not cheer up Robin, and she was depressed when she met the policemen at a café in the closest town to Black Oaks.

Sergeant Pine had suggested the café as a meeting place, because he assumed that Robin would be hungry after her long ride. Robin didn't have much of an appetite, but she wolfed down a hamburger and finished a cup of black coffee to fortify her for the ordeal to come.

"Did you ever figure out who ordered the knife?" Robin asked.

"It was made at a novelty shop in Wisconsin, but the owner was paid in cash, and he sent the box and knife to a post office box in Hood River. No one at the post office remembers who picked up the package."

"I have a good idea who it was," Robin said, and while she ate, Robin explained how she had figured out who had murdered Frank Melville and Justin Trent. By the time the sergeant and the detectives were ready to accompany Robin to Black Oaks, she had convinced them that the person they were going to arrest was guilty of a double homicide.

The ride up Solitude Mountain was an easy journey that afternoon. With clear skies, Robin should have enjoyed the scenic views, but all she could think about was how sad she would be on the journey back to Portland.

Sergeant Pine had called ahead, and the gate swung open shortly after he announced his presence over the intercom. Sheila Monroe was waiting at the front door when the sergeant, the detectives, Robin, and a car with a male and female deputy parked out front.

"Has there been a break in the case?" Sheila asked.

"There has," Pine answered. "May we come in?"

"Of course. Follow me. Nelly is in the library."

Robin and the policemen followed Sheila along the corridor past the tapestry depicting the wolf hunt.

"Nelly, the police and Robin are here," Sheila said as she opened the library door.

Nelly was sitting in one of the comfortable chairs that bracketed the fireplace, reading a novel. A fire heated the room. Nelly placed a bookmark between the pages and stood up.

"What brings you back to Black Oaks?" she asked.

"A few things. First, I wanted to tell you that Corey Rockwell has been arrested for murdering

Claire Winters, and Yousef Khan is going to be a free man."

"Oh my God!" Nelly exclaimed. "That's fantastic. How did you manage that?"

"I didn't. My investigator is the hero in this story. He cracked Rockwell's alibi by getting Tony Clark to confess that Rockwell left his bungalow to murder Claire Winters. Clark told the police that he walked back and forth in front of the window that faced Rose McIntire's bungalow putting a black wig on and taking it off to make it look like Rockwell was with him."

"Dad would have been so happy. Thank you, Robin."

"There's another reason we're here," Sergeant Pine said.

"Miss Lockwood thinks she knows who killed your father and Mr. Trent."

"Have you made an arrest?" Nelly asked.

"Not yet. We wanted to talk to you and Miss Monroe before we did anything."

"Please," Nelly said. "How can we help?"

"I'm trying to figure out something that happened right after we discovered your father in the elevator," Robin said.

Nelly paled. "I don't like thinking about that."

"I know. Can you try?"

"Definitely, if it will help find the man who murdered Justin and my father."

"Thanks. Now, I remember hearing the alarm bell and going onto the landing. Then I dropped onto the top of the elevator, opened the escape hatch, and lowered myself into the car. Do you remember what you and Sheila did after you heard the alarm?"

"We ran up from the first floor."

"Right. I could see you through the bars. You started to go into the car, but I stopped you."

Nelly nodded. "You said the elevator was a crime scene, and you didn't want anyone to contaminate it."

"After that, everyone except you, me, and Victor Zelko went down to the library. Am I right?"

"Yes."

"That's when you reminded me that the road to Black Oaks was blocked by mudslides, and we couldn't know when the police would be able to get here. Then you said we had to take your father's body out of the elevator."

"That's what I remember."

"And you said someone should take pictures of the elevator before we moved your father, so there would be a record for the police. That's when I went to my room to get my cell phone, so I could show photos to the police of the elevator as we'd found it."

Nelly nodded.

"You and Zelko were standing near the elevator when I came back, a minute or so later, right?"

"Yes," Nelly said.

"Did Zelko enter the cage while I was getting my phone?"

"No. He stayed where he was."

"But you did go into the elevator," Robin said.

"What do you mean?" Nelly said.

"When I dropped into the elevator, your father had Sheila's shawl draped over his shoulders. I pushed it to the floor of the car, so I could see his chest. When I returned with my cell phone, you were holding the shawl, so you must have gone into the elevator."

"You're right. I forgot. The shawl was on the floor, and I wanted to give it back to Sheila."

Robin got out her cell phone and showed Nelly the pictures she'd taken.

"I read the police reports. When the people from the crime lab examined the elevator, they didn't find anything in it. My pictures also show that the cage was empty after your dad was wheeled out."

Nelly and Sheila studied the pictures on the cell phone screen.

"It's empty," Sheila agreed.

"That's the problem," Robin said. "When I dropped into the cage, my foot hit a small piece of pipe. I saw it roll across the cage. But there's no sign of the pipe in my pictures or any mention in the police reports."

Robin looked at Nelly. "Since you were the only person who went into the car, you must have taken it."

Nelly looked confused. "I didn't take anything other than the shawl. And why would I take a piece of pipe?"

"Maybe it rolled onto the landing when you moved the wheelchair," Sheila said.

Robin showed them pictures of the landing.

"It's not there."

"Maybe you just thought there was a piece of pipe," Nelly said. "My dad's wheelchair took up most of the car, so you wouldn't have been able to see much of the floor. You might have hit one of the chair wheels and thought you hit something else."

"I definitely saw the pipe, and there's other evidence that proves it existed."

"What evidence?" Sheila asked.

"This might upset you," Robin said. "It's Mr. Melville before we took him out of the elevator. I can tell what it shows, if you don't want to see the picture."

Sheila looked sick. "Please, just tell us what's in the picture that's so important."

"Okay. There's a small, circular indentation on Mr. Melville's forehead that would match the end of the piece of pipe I saw."

"I'm really confused," Nelly said. "How does this pipe help us figure out who killed my father?"

"I just told you that Corey Rockwell was under arrest for killing Claire Winters."

"Yes."

"A couple of days ago, my investigator and I were discussing the case, and he said that Rockwell's scheme to have Tony Clark alibi him by going back and forth in front of his window with and without a black wig took a lot of planning. That made me think about your father's murder.

"I think you'd agree that creating a locked-room murder in an elevator stuck between floors isn't something you could come up with on the spur of the moment. Especially when it involved a dagger with a werewolf handle made of silver. You'd have to have the knife made well in advance of using it."

"That makes sense," Sheila said.

"Once I figured that out, I was able to eliminate several people as suspects. Corey Rockwell was invited to come to Black Oaks just before your father was murdered. He'd probably never heard of Mr. Melville or the Black Oaks legend. Even if he researched it, he wouldn't have had the time to get the knife made. Then there's motive. When Rockwell arrived at Black Oaks he didn't have a reason to want to kill Mr. Melville. He thought your father was going to finance a picture for him.

"Jose Alvarez had a motive to kill your father, but he was locked up on death row until a few days before he was invited to Black Oaks, so he couldn't have had the knife made, even assuming that he even knew about the legend of Black Oaks.

"Then there's the elevator. Neither Jose nor Corey Rockwell knew there was an elevator at Black Oaks until they arrived, so they wouldn't have had any way of planning the locked-cage murder.

"Victor Zelko was also locked up until the evening of the crime. We know Luther told him about Black Oaks, but would he have described the elevator in detail? And how would Zelko get the knife?

"Once I thought it out, I realized that the person who murdered Frank Melville had to have intimate knowledge of the way the elevator worked and had to know about the Black Oaks curse and Mr. Melville's fear of it. That left you, Sheila, Mrs. Raskin, Luther, and Justin Trent."

"I still don't understand what the pipe has to do with anything," Sheila said.

"It's the key to how Mr. Melville was murdered. As soon as I measured the circumference of the knife handle, I realized that the knife couldn't fit between the bars of the cage. That meant that the killer had to be inside the elevator when Mr. Melville was stabbed. What no one could figure out was how the killer could get out of the elevator when it was stopped between the second and third floor."

"You got in through the escape hatch. Why couldn't the killer get out that way?" Sheila asked.

"It's a possibility, but I eliminated three of the people on the third-floor landing, Corey Rockwell, Zelko, and Jose. That leaves Justin Trent, and, for reasons I will explain, I'm certain he did not kill your father.

"Finally, you two didn't see anyone running down or up the stairs."

"So, how did the murderer get out?" Sheila asked.

"The killer was never in the elevator when it went up," Robin answered.

"I'm confused," Nelly said.

"You shouldn't be, since you murdered your father."

Nelly's cheeks burned red with rage.

"That's a disgusting thing to say. I loved my father."

"You're the only person who could have killed Mr. Melville."

Nelly folded her arms across her chest and glared at Robin.

"Why don't you tell everyone how I killed my father when I was in the hall when the elevator went up."

"Your plan was brilliant. You knew your father

believed in the Black Oaks curse, and you decided to frighten him with the box with the pentagram and the knife with the silver werewolf handle. During dinner, you went into the kitchen to order drinks for everyone. There is a door from the kitchen into the main hall. We talked to the caterers. They remember you coming into the kitchen with the drink orders, then going into the hall and returning. That's when you put the box with the knife in the hall for Mrs. Raskin to find.

"When your father reacted to the knife as you thought he would, you made sure he went into the library, and you brought the box with the knife there. When your father was calmer, you told everyone to go to bed.

"Next, you had to get Sheila away from you and your father, so you told her to get Mr. Melville's brandy. That's when you pulled your magic trick. It was brilliant, but we were able to duplicate it using a computer simulation.

"You'd taken the knife out of the box at some point. As soon as your father was in the elevator, you stabbed him in the heart. Death would have been instantaneous. Then you pressed in the Stop/Alarm button with one end of the pipe and kept it in place by wedging it against your father's forehead. When that was done, you pressed the button for the third floor.

"The first time I came to Black Oaks, Mrs. Raskin took me to the third floor in the elevator. She pressed the button, but the car didn't move. She explained that I had to shut the gate or the car wouldn't go up. You pressed the third-floor button, stepped out of the elevator, and closed the gate. As the elevator rose, you hurried back to the hall just before Sheila came out of the kitchen.

"The first time I went up in the elevator, it jerked to a stop for a moment between the second and third floors hard enough for me to lose my balance. Mrs. Raskin said it did that frequently, and she'd asked your father to fix it. You knew the elevator would jerk when it was halfway between the second and third floor. When it did, your father was thrown back in his chair, the pipe fell to the floor, the Stop/Alarm was activated, and the elevator came to a halt."

"Wow. That's some theory, but it's all speculation."

"Not really," Robin said. "Someone in Black Oaks killed your father. I've already eliminated Jose, Zelko, and Rockwell. The caterers, Mrs. Raskin, and Luther didn't have a motive and were nowhere near the elevator when your father was killed. Justin may have had a motive, since he loved you, but he was nowhere near the elevator when your father was killed, and Sheila was in the kitchen getting the brandy, so she couldn't have killed your father. That leaves only one person, you. And you were the only person who went in the elevator when the piece of pipe went missing."

"You're forgetting one thing, Robin. I loved my father. I sacrificed everything to be with him after my mom died and he was injured. And Justin and I were planning to marry. What possible motive could I have for killing the two most important people in my life?"

"That was the hardest thing to figure out, but I

have. Justin Trent specialized in probate at his law firm. He would be the person your father consulted if he wanted to change his will. Justin and your father had a meeting when he came to Black Oaks, but no one else was at it. Any notes about that meeting would have been on Justin's laptop or phone, and they've gone missing. I think that the person who killed Justin got rid of the laptop and phone. I'm willing to bet that they're somewhere in the woods around Black Oaks, and I'm willing to bet that the person who buried them in those woods knew about ways to get out of the manor without being seen, which would require a knowledge of the secret passages in the manor house.

"Justin was in love with you, Nelly. He would have told you that your father was going to marry Sheila and make her his beneficiary. I'm guessing that you felt your father had betrayed you after everything you'd done for him. You left Oxford and became his full-time caregiver. As you just said, you sacrificed your life to help him."

"What are you talking about?" Nelly said. "I didn't know about the marriage until Dad announced it at dinner. How did I manufacture that knife between Dad's announcement and his murder?"

"I think you knew about the marriage and the will well before that dinner. Your father called Justin to tell him that he was going to marry Sheila and wanted to change his will a month and a half before he was murdered. The police subpoenaed Justin's notes. They also have phone records showing that your fa-

ther called him from Black Oaks, and Justin called
you soon after.

"Justin loved you and he told you that you were going to be cut out of your inheritance. That's why Justin had to die after you killed Mr. Melville. Everyone
thought you loved your father, and no one could think
of a motive you might have for killing him or Justin.
Only Justin could supply the motive. He would never
have suspected that he was in danger when you asked
to meet him in the basement. That's why there were
no defense wounds."

"This is complete nonsense," Nelly said. "I loved
Justin and I loved my father."

"I'm afraid we're at the point in this case where a
jury will have to decide whether you hated them more
than you loved them," Sergeant Pine said. "Right now,
I'm placing you under arrest for the murder of Frank
Melville and Justin Trent. Anything you say can be
held against you . . ."

Robin tuned out the sergeant while he gave Nelly
the rest of the Miranda warnings. She should have felt
proud of herself for solving a case this complex. Instead, she felt awful.

EPILOGUE

SEVERAL MONTHS LATER

Robin had been tied up in trial on Monday and Tuesday, so she hadn't been able to write a brief that had to be filed in the Oregon Court of Appeals by the end of the week. She was banging away on her computer keyboard when Loretta walked into her office.

The guilt phase of Nelly Melville's trial for aggravated murder had lasted three weeks, and Robin had been a witness. After the jury handed down a guilty verdict, the sentencing phase had started. It had lasted a week, and Loretta had been following it.

"I just heard. The jury voted for life with the possibility of parole, so no death sentence."

"That's a relief."

"You don't think she deserved to be on death row?"

"I know Nelly killed two people, but I can't help feeling sorry for her. She did give up everything to live in that awful place and take care of her father. Then he falls in love and decides to leave everything to Sheila Monroe. I can see how she would feel betrayed."

"It doesn't excuse what she did."

"No, it doesn't."

Loretta sat in one of the client chairs. "Do you believe in curses?"

"No. I believe life is weird, and odd things happen all the time."

"Still, everyone who has ever lived at Black Oaks was met with tragedy. There are the McTavishes and Ian and Alice Standish at the original manor house, and Frank, Katherine, and Nelly Melville at the copy. You could also count Sheila Monroe as a victim because she lost her fiancé, and there's Justin Trent."

"You make a good point. I'm just too rational to believe in the supernatural."

"What will happen to Black Oaks?"

"I don't have any idea. I heard that Nelly tried to sell it to use for her legal fees, but I don't think there have been any offers."

"I haven't seen the place, but, from the way you and Ken have described it, you'd have to be a real oddball to want to live there."

"Amen to that," Robin agreed.

Loretta shook her head. "What a tragedy. Look at how many lives were ruined."

"There is one happy ending," Robin said. "Jose Alvarez called. He's enrolled in a paralegal program at Portland Community College. He's even talking about going to law school. And the Innocence Project has asked him to be the keynote speaker at their annual fundraiser. They've also found him a part-time job at their office."

"Will it be enough to live on?"

"No. Nelly reneged on her promise to help Jose, but I've given him the fee Nelly gave us to work on Corey Rockwell's case and the money Frank Melville gave us to get him out of prison. It should be enough to tide him over for a while."

"A life for a life," Loretta said. "Nelly is in, and Jose is out. There's some justice in that."

"Not much," Robin said sadly.

"At least there was something good that's come out of this mess. That's better than a lot of what happens in a lot of our cases."

"But it is what keeps us going," Robin answered. "And now, I've got to get back to this brief in hopes that there may be one more happy ending."

ACKNOWLEDGMENTS

A writer has his name in big letters on the front of his book, but writing a novel is a collaborative effort. Keith Kahla, my editor, beat me up until I rewrote my not-so-good first draft until it passed inspection. Ryan Jenkins, my copyeditor, combed the new draft for grammatical and other mistakes, then Hector De-Jean, Martin Quinn, Alice Pfeifer, Kelley Ragland, Sally Richardson, Ken Silver, David Rotstein, Matie Argiropoulos, and Theresa Plummer, the voice of Robin Lockwood, got together on various aspects of publishing to produce the book you just read or the audio book to which you just listened.

None of this would have happened if Jennifer Weltz, my brilliant agent, and the team at the Jean V. Naggar Literary Agency had not placed *Murder at Black Oaks* at St. Martin's; Pat Wheeler and Jake Pavkov hadn't answered technical questions about phone lines and street fighting; and my wife, Melanie Nelson, had not given me her love and support. Thanks also to my daughter, Ami; my son, Daniel; his wife, Amanda; and my two fabulous grandkids, Loots and Marissa, for making my life so much fun.

Finally, thanks to Ellery Queen, Agatha Christie, John Dickson Carr, Erle Stanley Gardner, and all the other mystery writers old and new who have given me so much enjoyment over the years.

Read on for an excerpt from
Betrayal—
the next exciting novel by Phillip Margolin, available soon in hardcover from Minotaur Books!

Shortly before Megan Radcliffe's favorite show started, a very odd event occurred that was followed by a horrifying event.

The show started at 8:00, so Megan walked to her kitchen at 7:50 to make a snack. To get to the kitchen, she passed a window that looked across the street at the home of Margaret and Nathan Finch and their two children, Annie and Ryan. Megan saw a woman pounding on the Finches' front door. She was shouting, but Megan couldn't hear what the woman was saying.

Megan watched for a moment. Then she went to the kitchen, fixed some cheese and crackers, and headed back to the living room. She had taped the show, so she wasn't worried about missing any of it. At some time between 8:05 and 8:10, she passed the window again and saw the woman leave the porch and walk away from the Finches' house. That was the odd event. Megan's show paused for a commercial at 8:15, and she looked out the window in her living room that faced the Finch house. The light from the Finches' living room illuminated the porch, but no one was on it. At 8:30, when her show ended, Megan heard a car stop across the street. She recognized Arthur Proctor, who taught English at Marie Curie Middle School, walking to the Finches' front door. She saw him ring the bell, then she saw him go inside. She had finished her snack, and then took her plate to the kitchen. When she returned to the living room, she saw Proctor bolt out of the Finch house, leaving the front door wide open.

Megan opened her front door and walked toward the teacher. He looked horrified.

"What happened?" Megan shouted. Proctor waved her away. He had his phone out and was shouting into it. This is what Megan heard:

"911. What is your emergency?"

"They're all dead."

"Sir, who am I speaking with?"

"Sorry, I'm just . . . I'm Annie's teacher, Arthur Proctor. I came to the house to talk about Annie's scholarship, and I found them."

"Found who?"

"Everyone. The Finch family. They're all dead."

PART TWO

MEET THE FINCHES

TEN YEARS LATER

Lloyd Standish was as American as apple pie, if the pie was moldy and inedible. The black sheep in a family whose ancestors had come over on the *Mayflower,* Lloyd had blond hair, a Roman nose, and blue eyes that screamed WASP, and he didn't contain a single strand of DNA linking him to any state in the disbanded USSR. That, and a sociopathic personality, were the reasons that Jack Kovalev, who ran the Russian mob in Oregon, had made Lloyd his right-hand man. Standish could mingle with a class of people who would never associate with a Slavic mobster. He also had no qualms about getting his hands very dirty. In truth, Lloyd enjoyed tasks that involved violence.

Tonight, Lloyd was watching a torrential rain inundate a supermarket parking lot as he waited to send a prize piece of trailer trash on a mission that would net his boss several thousand dollars. Twenty minutes after he was supposed to arrive, Otis Truax parked his car on the edge of the lot. Lloyd raised his umbrella and walked through a row of cars to the driver's window. Truax was a scrawny, unemployed nobody with mousy brown hair, watery brown eyes, and outstanding debts to loan sharks, which made him the perfect recruit for the mob's staged auto accident insurance scam.

Truax lowered the driver's-side window a crack, leaning away from the drops that the unruly wind swept into his car. Lloyd stared at Truax until Truax looked away.

"You're late, Otis," Standish said, his tone reeking of menace.

"Sorry. Traffic," Truax mumbled.

"I do not appreciate having to stand outside in a fucking downpour for twenty minutes because you can't tell time. And I definitely do not like people who apologize for fucking up. Are you weak, Otis? Are you a fuckup?"

"No," Truax said.

"Speak up, Otis. Are you someone I can count on? Because you are being entrusted with a very important mission. If you accomplish this mission, your debt to certain vicious degenerates will be taken care of. Are you going to complete your mission and get your reward, or do you want to beg off and have many bones in your body broken?"

Despite the chill in the air, Truax was sweating. "You can count on me, Mr. Standish," Truax said.

Lloyd smiled. "Of course I can. You're my man,

Otis. I wouldn't have selected you if I didn't have complete faith in you. So, are you ready to go?"

"Yeah, but are you sure about this?"

"Of course. It'll be a piece of cake. We have it down to a science. There's a spotter. He'll tell you when the mark is headed into the intersection. Then you smash into the side of the vehicle. We have a doctor who'll say you're injured, a lawyer who deals with the insurance company, and an insurance agent who's in our pocket. You just crash the car, and we'll take care of you."

"What if the cops don't believe me?"

"Not a problem. Didn't I tell you that we supply witnesses who'll claim our mark was speeding or ran a red light?"

"Yeah, that's what you said. But what if I really get hurt? This rain is coming down hard."

"Hey, Otis, you know how to drive a car, right?"

"Yeah," Truax answered hesitantly.

"Then fasten your seat belt, and let's get you a payday."

Alan Chen decided that he would call out, "Free at last, Lord, free at last," when he walked in the door. He was sure that would get a laugh out of Susan. And it was completely true. They had a two-week vacation at an all-inclusive resort in Mexico, and he planned to spend every waking hour sipping piña coladas on the beach and not looking at anything that had a number in it.

Alan pulled into the driveway and was surprised that the house was dark. Susan was usually home before he got in, but he wasn't worried. His wife worked as a trial assistant at a law firm and might have had things to wrap up before she could leave on their vacation.

Alan took off his shoes when he entered the house. Then he went into the bedroom and put on a T-shirt and sweatpants. After he changed, he walked into the living room and looked out at the front of the house to see if Susan had come home yet. When he didn't see her car, Alan walked into the kitchen and started to fix dinner.

He enjoyed his job as a CPA, but he had been working long hours and he couldn't wait to unwind in Cabo. They'd bought a New York steak to celebrate, and Alan took it out of the freezer. While he waited for it to thaw, he prepared their salad.

Susan still wasn't home when he started working on the baked potatoes. Alan checked his watch. It was almost six. He frowned. What could be keeping her? He took out his phone and called Susan. The call went to voice mail, so he dialed her office. She didn't pick up, so he dialed her best friend at the office, hoping that she was still in.

"Hi, Tina," he said when he was connected. "Is Susan still working?"

"No. She left around five, Alan."

"Did she say she was going somewhere other than home?"

Tina laughed. "She was definitely headed home. All she's been talking about is your vacation."

Tina suddenly understood why Alan was calling, and her light tone changed to concern.

"Isn't she home yet?"

"No."

"She probably stopped off to get some sunscreen," Tina said.

Alan laughed, but he was worried. And his anxiety increased with each passing minute. Alan tried Susan's cell phone again, with the same result. Then he peered through the drops beating on the living room window, willing her car to appear. It didn't, so he went back to the kitchen. He was putting the baked potatoes in the oven when the doorbell rang.

Alan hurried to the front door and opened it. Two men were standing on the welcome mat. One man was wearing a yellow slicker over a policeman's uniform, and the other man was tall, thin, and balding and he was wearing a raincoat over a brown suit.

"Yes?" Alan asked, afraid of what he might hear.

"I'm Chet Marx," the man in plainclothes said as he held up his identification. "I'm a detective with the Portland police. This is Ronald Jefferson. Can we come in?"

Alan had been oblivious to the rain that was pounding on the two men until they asked to enter his house. He stepped back.

"Of course. Come in," he said.

"Are you related to Susan Chen?" Detective Marx asked.

"I'm her husband, Alan."

Marx looked at the living room. "I think you should sit down," he said.

"Why? What's this about?"

"We have some very bad news, sir. It would be better if you were sitting when you heard it."

"Is this . . . Is it Susan?"

Marx nodded, and Alan collapsed on the nearest chair. The detective took a seat opposite Alan. Jefferson stood off to one side.

"Your wife was in a traffic accident," Marx said.

"Is she in the hospital?" Alan asked, hoping that the detective would say she was.

"I'm afraid she passed," Marx said.

Alan stared at Marx for a second. Then his chest heaved, and he began to cry. The detective waited until Alan stopped sobbing.

"There's something else you need to know," Marx said. "We think that the accident that killed your wife was staged as part of an insurance scam."

Alan's head jerked up. "What?"

"There are organized groups who stage accidents to collect insurance money. It's unusual for there to be a fatality, but this time . . ."

Marx let the sentence hang.

"Someone murdered Susan?" Alan asked.

"We think so. We have the driver of the other car in custody, and I want to assure you that we are going to make the people responsible for your wife's death pay."

Alan didn't respond. He had stopped crying, and he was looking past the policemen.

"The district attorney may contact you. He might need you as a witness. But it's too early to tell. Meanwhile, we need you to come with us to identify your wife. Do you feel up to it?"

Alan nodded.

"I'm sorry to put you through this," Marx apologized.

"I understand. Let me change."

"Of course."

Alan headed for the bedroom, and Jefferson shook his head.

"Poor bastard."

Marx sighed. "I don't know how many times I've done this. It never gets easier."

Margaret Finch, attorney-at-law, was almost six feet tall, with cheerleader hair she dyed blond, blue eyes that were made bluer by contacts, and a slender, toned body that had been manufactured by personal trainers in upscale gyms and maintained by a vegetarian diet. She might have been more attractive if her face was a little fuller, but plastic surgery had given it a pinched appearance that struck people as a little bit off. Margaret also put people off because she rarely smiled. That was a product of being under constant stress, because of the work she did and the people who paid her for this work.

Lloyd Standish had summoned Margaret to a meeting a little before midnight. Meetings with the mobster outside normal office hours rarely involved anything good, but given the size of the retainer Jack Kovalev paid her, she had no choice but to get dressed and drive downtown in the dark in the middle of an unsettling downpour.

What was as unsettling as the manic rain and having to meet Standish, who gave her the creeps, was having to meet him in a seedy bar owned by Kovalev. The usual place for a meeting with Standish was one of the upscale restaurants where he preferred to dine.

Three things occurred to Margaret as soon as she entered the bar. First, Standish, who usually dressed like a banker, was wearing jeans, a dark baseball cap, and a gray sweatshirt under a black raincoat. Second, he was sitting in a booth in the back of the bar, where the lighting was dim. Three, he had summoned Margaret to a meeting in the middle of the night. It didn't take Sherlock Holmes to deduce that something had gone horribly wrong. That didn't keep Margaret from being annoyed.

"Why the cloak-and-dagger scenario, Lloyd?" Margaret asked as she slipped onto the seat across from Standish. "Is there some reason we couldn't meet during office hours like civilized people?"

"I'm in no mood for impertinence, Margaret. You're paid to do what we tell you to do, when we tell you. So, stow the attitude. There was a very bad screwup tonight. One of our drivers killed a woman."

"Jesus!"

"The man's name is Otis Truax. He's in custody, and he is spineless. You are going to go to the jail right now and shut him up before he cuts a deal to save his worthless skin."

"What happened? I need some background before I see him."

"I wasn't at the scene, but one of our people told me Truax was going way too fast. The roadway was slick, he went into a skid, and he may have hit the accelerator instead of the brake. He T-boned the other car. Hit it right in the driver's door. The car was totaled, and the driver died at the scene."

"What about Truax? Why is he in jail instead of the hospital?"

Standish laughed. "If the asshole had died, it would have saved me a lot of trouble, but all he walked away with were a few bruises."

"I told you this insurance scam was risky," Margaret said.

"Maybe you were right, but we're not going to be Monday-morning quarterbacks right now. What you are going to do is damage control. Shut up Truax and bail him out."

"Then what? There was a death. The DA is going to have Truax over a barrel. They'll know he was a tool, and they'll offer him a sweetheart deal to get him to roll over. How am I going to keep him from talking after I get him out?"

The look Standish gave her made Margaret's stomach roll.

"Let me worry about that problem. You take care of business right now."

Standish slapped a twenty on the table and left. Margaret waited to leave so they wouldn't be seen together. While she waited, she wished she'd ordered a stiff drink. Even the crap they probably served in this dump would have helped calm her down and kept her from thinking about the future Otis Truax faced once he was free and unprotected by steel bars and jail guards.

Margaret drove to the Multnomah County Justice Center, an eighteen-story, concrete-and-glass building in downtown Portland. The building was home to the central precinct of the Portland Police Bureau, a branch of the Multnomah County District Attorney's Office, several courtrooms, and the Multnomah County Jail, which occupied the fourth through tenth floors.

The jail reception area was on the second floor. At this hour, there was almost no one around. Margaret walked through the building's vaulted lobby, past curving stairs that led to the courtrooms, and through a glass door. She showed her ID to the duty officer and went through a metal detector before taking an elevator to the floor where attorneys met their clients.

Margaret walked out of the elevator into a narrow, concrete hallway whose walls were painted pastel yellow. There was a thick metal door at one end. She pressed the button on the intercom and announced her presence. Moments later, she heard the electronic locks snap, and a guard opened the door and escorted her down another narrow hallway that ran in front of three contact visiting rooms. She could see into the rooms through large windows outfitted with shatterproof glass.

The guard stopped in front of a solid metal door

that opened into the first visiting room. Molded plastic chairs stood on either side of a metal table that was bolted to the floor. Moments after the guard shut the door to the hallway, a second door in the room's other wall opened and Otis Truax shuffled into the visiting room.

The first words that sprang into Margaret's mind when she saw her client were *pathetic* and *pitiful*. Truax swam in his orange jail-issued jumpsuit. His shoulders were hunched, and, when he raised his eyes from the floor, Margaret could see that they were red-rimmed from crying.

"My name is Margaret Finch, and I'm going to represent you."

"I ain't got any money, Mrs. Finch."

Margaret smiled in a way that she hoped would gain Truax's confidence.

"That's not a problem. You have friends who are going to take care of you."

"You mean—"

Margaret raised her hand to cut him off. "No need to mention names when we don't know if anyone is listening to our conversation, is there?"

"No, ma'am."

"Good. Tomorrow, I'm going to be by your side in court, and I'm going to ask the judge to set bail for you. You don't have to worry; bail will be posted for you, no matter how much the court requires. So, you'll be out of here sometime tomorrow."

"Thank you."

"Until then, there's only one thing you have to do. Do you know what that is?"

Truax's brow furrowed, and Margaret could almost see the rusted wheels in his tiny brain turning slowly. After a few moments, Truax gave up.

"I don't know the answer," he confessed.

Margaret smiled warmly. "It's something you'll be able to do easily, Otis. May I call you Otis?"

"Yeah."

"What you have to do is nothing. And by that I mean, you have to keep your mouth shut. No talking to guards, inmates, or anyone else about what happened last night. If anyone tries to talk to you, you will say these simple words: 'I will only talk when my attorney is with me.' Do you think you can remember that sentence?"

Truax's head bobbed up and down.

"Good," Margaret said. "Why don't you repeat it back to me. I'm a guard and I say, 'Hey, Mr. Truax, what happened in that accident?' What do you say?"

"I ain't saying a word unless my attorney is with me."

Margaret beamed. "Excellent."

"Uh, I did have a question."

"Yes, Otis?"

"When they arrested me, there was this detective. He said I could be charged with murder and go to jail for the rest of my life. But he also said that I could make a deal that might keep me out of jail if I told them who told me to make the accident."

Margaret struggled to keep the smile on her face. "What did you say to that?"

"What Mr.—"

Margaret held up her hand.

"Yeah, right," Truax said as he nodded up and down rapidly. "I said I wanted to talk to a lawyer."

"That's great, Otis. You did the right thing."

"Sure, but I don't want to get charged with murder. So, do you think I should take the deal?"

"That's a complicated question to answer, Otis, because we don't know the details of the deal. So, my suggestion, as your attorney, is that we get you out of jail first. When you're out of here, I'll talk to the DA and get the details of the deal. Then we can discuss it in my office, after you've gotten a good night's sleep. How does that sound?"

"It makes sense."

"Do you have any other questions?"

"Not right now."

"Good." Margaret stood up and pressed the button that summoned the guard. "You hang tight, and I'll see you in court real soon."